FRAGMENTS

MALCOLM HOLLINGDRAKE

Book Ten in the Harrogate Crime Series

Also by Malcolm Hollingdrake

Bridging the Gulf

Shadows from the Past
Short Stories for Short Journeys

The Harrogate Crime Series

Only the Dead

Hell's Gate

Flesh Evidence

Game Point

Dying Art

Crossed Out

The Third Breath

Treble Clef

Threadbare

Dedicated to

Sue, Rachel and Anna Clark.

Much loved family

In memory

Anthony Clark

my friend and brother-in-law

04/08/1959 – 09/01/2021

When you have eliminated all which is impossible, then whatever remains, however improbable, must be the truth.

Arthur Conan Doyle

Prologue

The invitation had been sitting on the mantelpiece since she had lodged it there after printing it from the website. Why she had performed both of those actions still confused her, it somehow seemed instinctive. Sipping the large glass of Merlot, she stared at it as if playing a game to see if she would look away before the print was bleached from the paper.

Melanie Masters had never liked reunions. Her first taste had been an annual college 'bash' some thirty years after her final year of students had all flown the academic nest. They had moved to various locations around the country with an eagerness and enthusiasm born from the naivety of youth. It was their new-found belief that they were now fully equipped to bring wisdom to the masses of eager pupils – soon, however, there would be the realisation that this was purely misguided missionary zeal. The thought of returning to Edge Hill College of Education, positioned on the edge of Ormskirk in Lancashire, for a weekend in August had not made her pulse race. It had, however, prompted her to ask the questions: Why? For what possible, sane reason should I attend?

Looking back was, to Melanie, anathema. She always argued strongly that returning to the past broke her concentration of where her future lay. "It's like constantly looking in your rear-view mirror when driving. You'll either come a cropper or become totally lost." This became her stock answer when responding to the written invitations that dropped onto the mat before the internet messages replaced them. At least then the invitation was on card, the college crest proud and prominent. Someone had also spent the time to write your name in a faux copperplate hand. They had taken trouble and gave the impression that they genuinely wanted you to be present. Why she had changed her mind she would never know. Maybe it was just in a moment of weakness – or more likely drunkenness – but it was still an acceptance. She felt regret of course and thought it was a huge mistake at the same time organising the hotel and planning the trip. Somewhere inside she felt a curiosity to see just how well her old friends and acquaintances had done. For one, she had prospered and had nothing to hide.

It could not be denied that arriving in Ormskirk had stimulated a flutter of the metaphorical wings trapped within her stomach. It was exciting to see those attending. Visions of the last days before their final departure all those years ago surfaced; the specific part of that year was now mysteriously manoeuvred into her mind's eye like a slide show. Many of those images brought a chuckle, each refreshed a memory, both good and bad. She had taken some photographs with her to be used as an icebreaker if nothing else, fished out of a box trawled from the back of the wardrobe. On flicking through the pile, they brought back memories. The names surprisingly returned to match the faces. She spoke out loud. "Goodness, yes, that's Christine Nisbet. Paul Wathen … did you marry?" She lifted a finger to her lip in the hope it would help her remember.

"… Annette, I think it was? Yes, it was and Janet Powell and there's Lesley Rawlinson." The names matched the photographs of the laughing friends as each was tossed back into the box. Looking back now she remembered the mixed feelings. At first, the warm, inner glow of nostalgia had contradicted all that she had imagined and feared about the visit but then, as the photographs were returned, that reassurance soon became short lived. Shaking her head, she sipped more wine.

At that first reunion Melanie watched as the gaggle, her gaggle, moved through the building. It was here, during the guided tour of the college, where the discomfort was rekindled. It felt as though she were not really present, as if she were an intruder. It was like some bizarre dream. After all, the college was a familiar place; it was a personal encyclopaedia of contradictory experiences and memories from her formative years. Maybe her past empiricism, the times of joy and laughter, tears and disappointment were all here, trapped and waiting to be flushed from the old walls and windows by the group's collective reminiscing – like Arthur emerging after hearing England's call in her hour of need.

Even the smell of the college was familiar she remembered, closing her eyes briefly which took her straight back to her student days. During this moment, she realised that she was on an imaginary road to Damascus and it was here she saw the light. It was not necessarily she who was at fault, but those who now surrounded her. They were the problem, the contradiction. Whilst her eyes were closed and she listened to the various voices tell familiar stories, she was back. They were the students she once knew so well, the friends she remembered, the peers she liked and trusted with her secrets, her hopes and desires, but when she opened her eyes and looked at each of the talking heads, they were not the same. These were strangers – imposters. Occasionally, a knowing glance or facial expression would rekindle the familiarity, bringing the past to the present, but they were brief. From that seemingly trapped moment in the long corridor, she vowed it would be her last ever reunion. She had, during that weekend, spent too long looking behind and she had emotionally crashed.

And then a chance letter arrived on a cold December morning which would change that intransigence. This was not a formal invitation, there was no RSVP, no copperplate hand, just a brief, handwritten note. It was the signature that drew Melanie's attention.

Norma Halsall taught in the same school in which Melanie had been appointed to serve out her probationary year. Although only a year or two older, Norma had offered guidance and support during the good and the bad periods of those anxious months. She had pointed out the possible mistakes new teachers make and through that voluntary, professional guidance, they had not only been colleagues, but had become staunch friends. After a year, Norma had moved school and Authority and they had eventually lost touch.

There had been no mention of the word *reunion* within the short, scribbled note; the proposal seemed more subtle and mature. It was suggested it would be more formal, an opportunity for like-minded retired teachers to share their experiences of life after the classroom and schools.

Beneath the signature there was also a list of people who had agreed to participate. It amounted to five not including Norma. All were female and all of a certain age. Melanie knew each one from either one school or another. It was surprising, once becoming an Advisory Teacher, just how many schools and therefore colleagues she had got to know.

Looking at the telephone number, a home one and not a mobile, she made up her mind to attend. After the first meeting she had immediately felt at home and the soirees, as they were soon entitled, were planned on a more frequent basis, each member taking it in turn to choose the venue. It seemed to suit them all. But now Melanie had received an invitation to an LEA reunion and this was an unwelcome surprise. Contrary to her vow, it had not been discarded but placed on the mantelpiece. Emptying the bottle into the glass she stood and picked up the invite again.

Chapter One

Even before Cyril arrived at West Park, he knew it would not be a promising start to his working day; he had a suspicion that he would find utter turmoil. The earlier cacophony of distant sirens had been a signal, not to summon the nearby cavalry but to sound the alarm that his day would not be the usual routine. He felt his morning demeanour tilt out of balance. To his growing annoyance, the wailing had been amplified on the light breeze as it carried the siren's sound, further funnelling it through the ginnel at the top of Robert Street and therefore ever closer. Although now quiet, the reflection of flashing blue on the layer of ceiling, like mist, gave a clue that an incident was still being dealt with and it beckoned him, that and his copper's instinct.

Closing the front door, he ensured he had everything he needed and went through the ritual mnemonic stopping at the word watch. He shook his wrist and checked the time again, a habit he had developed since old enough, reluctantly, to wear his first timepiece. He was later than usual. Julie had misplaced her car keys and the resulting search had brought further disruption and did not enhance his mood. He slipped the key into the lock whilst sensing the slight chill in the air; autumn was fast approaching. He raised his collar. A couple of neighbours were standing at their gates but he had no time for conversation let alone

1

gossip. Approaching the narrow passageway, he was dismayed to see the usual detritus left from the previous night. The small, shiny gas cylinders that seemed to be the latest favourite illicit youth pastime littered the left-hand side. From what he knew, they contained nitrous oxide, laughing gas, but Cyril was neither laughing nor amused. He kicked three to the side whilst grumbling to himself.

The morning mist was slowly being dragged from Harrogate's streets and open spaces. It was reluctant and dense. The warmth from the rising sun had initially seemed reticent to encourage stubborn elements to dissipate. It continued to cling to the upper structures, hiding and blurring the higher branches of some trees and the pinnacles of many of the taller buildings, in the process decapitating the sharp, needle spire of Trinity Methodist Church. For a while yet, the blue of the sky would remain hidden and lost. The sun, however, continued to fight valiantly and within the hour there would be little sign of the grey, organza veil other than the occasional damp, dewy area under the trees edging The Stray. For now, the only blue would be that of the flashing strobe lights emanating from the emergency vehicles, colouring the skin-like misty layer.

As always, accidents attract the attention of the passing public, those curious and inquisitive – this incident was sadly no different. It also brought DCI Cyril Bennett to a standstill as he emerged from the Robert Street passageway to be met by a group of bystanders. Assessing the scene, he quickly picked out the officers and medics. Although not there in an official capacity, the accident was directly and metaphorically blocking his route to work and his instinct to help and support enticed him. He noticed the familiar face of a road traffic officer and raised a hand. He received a swift nod and the raising of shoulders in reply.

It was the upturned pram that drew his initial curiosity followed by the sight of the young woman lying prostrate to the side of the road. Part of her body seemed broken over the edge of the kerb, and the irregular, deformed position of her limbs indicated the severity of her condition. Two paramedics were crouched over her. It was only then did Cyril spot the child. The medic, child in arms, stood a few feet away from the damaged pram and parent. To the right and wrapped in some wrought iron railings was the culprit, the car. The impact damage clearly demonstrated it had been travelling at considerable speed. The airbags, now deflated like limp ghosts, hung from the broken window giving an unrestricted view of the slumped driver. Cyril walked briskly across the road as another medic was just throwing a blanket over the car's roof, blocking the motionless driver from public scrutiny. As she did so she defensively turned her gaze towards Cyril, a look that flashed both her frustration and her anger which were clearly mapped on her features. Raising her hand, she signalled for him to stop and reinforced the request with a shake of her head.

Countering her move, he spoke. "DCI Bennett, police. Can I help?"

Shaking her head for a second time she bent to close the rucksack-type medical bag she had dropped in her haste.

"Nothing I can do for him. Might have been dead before impact." There was a short pause that enforced both the gravity of the situation and her frustration. "Dead, as is the young mother. Thank God the child doesn't have a scratch. Lives so tragically taken, vanished and gone in a split second – before our eyes just like this bloody morning mist." She tugged on the bag's strap clearly venting her angst.

Cyril turned and saw that the top of the spire was visible and the disc-like sun had broken through, transforming The Stray and its surrounds. There was now a clarity. The vista had magically moved from one of an Impressionist's canvas to that of a delicate and fine Bernard Evans watercolour. Momentarily, he admired the detail before turning back. He sensed her frustration and moved closer. "You said he was dead before impact?" Crouching, he looked directly at her and modified his tone seeing her distress. "You do what you can. You can do no more."

She failed to respond to his initial question. Her facial expression did not alter. She loaded the medical bag to her shoulder. It seemed to dwarf her petite, green-uniformed frame.

"True, but I'm trained to save life, not watch it fade in front of me." There was now even more anger in her tone, a certain defiance. She began to return to her vehicle.

"You mentioned that you thought the crash didn't kill the driver?"

She paused. "Considering the air bags, the seat belt and the damage to the car it's a presumption. The family and the police will know from the autopsy." Her tone, lightened, yet her frustration was still palpable. It appeared to him that her mood had mellowed as if in surrender. To Cyril she seemed barely a child herself.

Cyril stood to one side as she passed by before he moved to the front of the crashed car. The large piece of stone that centred the old metal railings gave the impression of leaning in the direction of the force but it had always faced that way. An historic relic from Harrogate's past, it identified the outer marker of the toll road; he passed it daily and knew it well. The railings, however, were totally mangled by the force of the collision. Looking back along the road towards the other two casualties, Cyril could see the car had demolished a roadside bench, a road sign and a single metal post before finally coming to rest in what looked like a catch net of wrought iron. Somewhere from the first collision to the car's final resting place, the woman and child had been collected in the melee.

Walking back down the road he noticed that the spectating public had been moved further away and a taped barrier put in place.

Approaching the casualty on the ground, he was just in time to watch the final attempts at CPR. He immediately thought of Julie. Things like this could happen to anyone at any time. This accident had taken but a second and he suddenly felt vulnerable and insignificant. The poor woman had set out that morning, probably kissed her husband before he left for work, and within the hour her life was no more, snuffed out so callously.

After a moment's reflection he raised his eyes heavenward and then turned to look at the remaining few people who were still congregated. Some were clearly animated having possibly witnessed the whole incident. Cyril walked over.

"Police. Anyone see the whole thing?" He addressed a group of four people.

Some shook their heads but a couple pointed in the direction of a mature lady sitting at one of the tables of the nearby roadside café. A foil blanket was wrapped around her shoulders and a small dog lay obediently across her lap. A female officer was with her stroking the dog's fine coat. The officer stood defensively as Cyril approached.

"DCI Bennett." He held his ID and she relaxed, resting a protective hand on the woman's shoulders.

"Ms Nicholson, Joan Nicholson, was here like she is most days. She walks her dog and then comes over for a coffee. She witnessed it all. Still a bit shaky but you can understand that. What of the mother?" As she asked, the PC turned to look as the body was being transferred to the rear of the ambulance.

Cyril shook his head which brought an immediate response to the face of the young officer. Her mouth contorted. She closed her eyes as her head and shoulders slumped.

"Make sure you get a full statement and then check any CCTV footage from these shops. This road will be closed for some time and the traffic will be dreadful. Has Ms Nicholson been checked by a paramedic?" Cyril's instruction was deliberately firm and the young officer quickly responded.

"Briefly, sir." She fingered the foil blanket. "He asked me to just keep an eye on her but she doesn't want any fuss or bother. She keeps assuring me she's fine!" The officer raised her face and forced a smile.

Cyril nodded. "Well done. It's not always easy this job."

He turned, crossing the now traffic-free West Park before walking down the footpath that would lead to Otley Road. He slipped an electronic cigarette between his lips and inhaled. It brought a degree of relief as the vapour poured out and over his lips, lingering before quickly disappearing behind him. It was still before ten. It was going to be a long day, a day he dreaded, one filled with meetings and budget justifications. He visualised the young paramedic's face, the moment she looked away from the driver's body and it seemed to haunt him.

A car horn stopped him in his tracks. He had stepped into the side road. The driver pointed to his own eyes and shook his head. Cyril mouthed the word *sorry* and raised a hand in apology. His heart was suddenly beating rapidly. *It takes but a second,* he thought before regaining his composure. Checking the road both ways, he crossed and nipped into the newsagent's to collect his daily paper.

Leaving the shop, he made a call detailing the reason for his delay, giving the registration number of the car in the accident and requesting owner information.

The day was going to be just as Cyril had predicted – long!

***

The workshop door was left ajar. To call it a workshop had always pushed the boundaries of imagination just that bit too far, as to many it was a shed. Like all non-living spaces in domestic properties, it was like the garage which no longer housed the car; so it was with the shed, the workshop, its original purpose had been lost over time. Space abhors a vacuum and this vacuum had been slowly filled to become a haven for those items which no longer seemed necessary or useful, but could not be thrown away as one day they might become so. The heavily stained, hardwood topped bench had come from a school near York when the science department was upgraded; the two stools from another. These, however, were clear and clean and had recently been used. What was once stored on the bench was now stacked nearer the corners. Maybe this could better be described as more of a magpie's nest. It brought the scientific term for the bird to mind, *Pica Pica.*

Picking up a cloth, the stools were wiped; a pointless exercise as they were spotlessly clean. For a few moments, a tired body perched on the one nearer the bench to contemplate the contents of the room.

In all honesty there was too much pica pica here, rescued over the years – and not just from one school either. Sometimes looking at the dust and cob-webbed covered collection of life and work souvenirs brought the same incredulity that all this was to be thrown out. Discarded, as the New National Curriculum brought about one syllabus change after another, or new headteachers or heads of departments felt the need to change something when budget constraints allowed. Unbelievably this very bench was judged inadequate! The wooden surface still felt smooth to the touch. It was acid proof, built like a tank and contained a good sink. The gas taps were still fixed on even though they were no longer connected. It was all perfectly functional but then new was needed. The staff making these decisions were like cats scenting or dogs pissing to mark out territory. Some people seem to have to make changes in order to stamp their mark, their authority, on the world. Consequently the old was replaced with furniture made from what looked like compressed cardboard, justified in the name of fashion or progress. That was criminal, reprehensible. It wasn't a crime to acquire these things; in fact they were being saved from going to landfill. Recycled and given a new home.

There was little feeling of satisfaction today though. Before the recent tidy the place was just a tip. Rather than being a work space, it had become a store space. On the upper shelf that ran down one wall there was a collection of amber-tinted glass bottles, sitting like triplets amongst paint tins, a mouse trap and car polish. Unlike everything else, these three were no longer dust-covered nor forlorn. Their titles could be easily read: Methanol, Benzine and Chloroform. Each name was etched onto an opaque rectangle on the bottles' faces. The only bottle where its contents remained was the last. These items were the only ones stolen, apparently removed from the chemistry cupboard at the Teachers' Centre where there was more than one set anyway and these particular ones were lost at the back of the store cupboard. The thief claimed not to be sorry as these bottles meant so much more to me. Adding the correct liquids and transporting them home was an action of rash selfishness. I imagine every teacher has something linked to their subject at home, if only a stick of chalk – the artist, the odd brush, the PE teacher, a whistle. Who really knows? Who truly cares?

Chapter Two

The room was dark, the blackness softened only by the faint glow of the green light from the clock to Cyril's left. There was no movement. The void only amplified the sound of the rain gurgling and spluttering within the gutter some distance above the open bedroom window. It seemed almost rhythmical, yet not in the least soporific; it was too intrusive. The sound of a speeding car echoed down West Park, wheels wet on tarmac, exhaust loud. It was the same piece of road where he had witnessed the tragic deaths the previous day.

Cyril looked across at Julie, her mouth slightly open, her hair fringing her forehead. She oozed warmth, cocooned within the covers. He watched her, scanning every inch of her face and feeling the warmth of her breath on his face. This intimate moment only heightened the thoughts that had troubled him since waking. The images had been clearly etched in his mind's eye of the paramedic, the collapsed driver and the young mother, a sight many should never have to witness. They appeared before him like still photographs, snapshots of puzzled faces, of pure grief.

Looking at the bedside clock, he knew he would sleep no more. Sliding from the bed he moved into the kitchen. The sound of the coffee machine competed with the gurgle of the rain. He swivelled his wedding ring round his finger and reflected briefly on the day Julie had accepted his proposal. It was as if it were a different time and place. Moving back to the bedroom door, coffee in hand, he looked at the slumbering figure. He watched as she stirred before settling again, her legs tucked tightly almost embryonically, the duvet pulled high covering her face. Nothing seemed to keep her from sleep and yet some of the things she witnessed on a daily basis would be enough to give the average human being nightmares.

"Sweet dreams," he mumbled before returning to the lounge and the paperwork he had left on the coffee table. One of the drawbacks of promotion was the increasing plethora of paperwork that seemed to expand year on year. It kept him away from the work he loved. It was as if technology had been designed, not to save on police time, but to add a further burden. Balancing what could be justified within any investigation was akin to a plate-spinning act. He sighed, sat back wrapping his hands around the hot coffee mug and focused on the painting displayed on the far wall. It was by Herbert Whone, his wedding present from Julie. The colours in the Impressionist's work seemed to echo the autumnal light as the orange from the setting sun licked the buildings and chimney as if giving a last protective sheath of warmth. The significance of the painting and the artist was not lost and it brought his mother's face into his mind's eye. As if by magic, he could hear the melodic strains of *The Lark Ascending*. Strangely, the moment's imagined music brought an end to his insomnia and he felt his eyes slowly turn leaden and close.

***

The sound of the alarm in some far-off place woke him and

to his surprise the half-full mug was still resting between his cupped hands.

"Cyril?" Julie came in, a large fleece dressing gown wrapped round her body. "What on earth are you doing in here?"

Cyril sighed and blew through his lips before rubbing his eyes with finger and thumb. "Couldn't sleep. All sorts coming and going in this tired mind of mine. That accident has really upset me. I normally can see a body, assess it and think nothing more of it but …"

"It would affect anyone, a young mother taken like that. It makes me realise how we should all live life to the full. As you know, I see things daily you shouldn't have to see but I'm trained and equipped for that professionally, psychologically and emotionally. We have strategies in place for coping with these pressures but even then, some things can still affect me, not often thankfully. One minute someone is laughing and joking and the next they're stretched out before me. Life is fragile, my darling man. Never forget it."

Cyril looked up as she leaned over to kiss the top of his head.

"The contents of that mug wouldn't be lost on Owen's desk. A fresh one and you need to eat," she whispered.

Cyril looked into the cup and a white halo-like ring swam on the surface of the coffee.

"You're wrong there." At the sink, he swilled the cup under the tap. "Owen would drink this if it were his!"

Julie pulled a face expressing her disgust. "We'll be doing the autopsy on the driver, your driver, today if all goes to plan. He's on Caner's list."

Dr Caner, like Julie, was one of the north east pathologists and she had worked alongside him for a number of years. Cyril remained silent, he simply tolerated Caner and had hoped that Julie would conduct the procedure. Being present at an autopsy did not agree with him. He had always held a dislike for bodily fluids, particularly his own, and to experience the sounds and sights of the specialist's instruments of body investigation left him both nauseous and traumatised.

"Seex. A Mr Paul Seex. Sex with an extra vitamin, that's how I remembered."

Julie laughed out loud before covering her mouth. "Sorry, I shouldn't laugh. You're a bad man, Bennett."

He smiled and winked. "I checked his car reg when I was walking to work after the crash. A heart attack they said. Just a second or two later and the young mother would've crossed the road safely. Discomforting that a single moment in time can mean the difference between living and dying. I shouldn't dwell too long on that thought."

***

The pick-up moved steadily down Langcliffe Avenue before slowing then stopping at the bridge. Within a second the passenger door opened and a smartly dressed elderly man moved towards the parapet. Leaning over, he held the plastic bag that concealed a wrapped package. Looking quickly along the road in both directions he let it fall before returning to the car. The process took less than thirty seconds.

Concealed within the packaging was a small, plastic square – a *Tile* – a tracking tag that would allow the package to be easily located using a mobile phone. It would also confirm collection.

***

As Cyril entered the open-plan office area, Detective Inspector David Owen was at his desk as were a number of other officers. Shakti looked around from behind her computer screen and waggled her fingers in an attempt at a wave. Cyril paused. Owen glanced and quickly removed his feet from the small filing cabinet positioned to the side of his cluttered desk. He smiled.

"Morning. Coffee, sir?"

"Make sure it's in a clean cup, Owen, and don't forget a saucer, one that matches the cup would be nice for once. Thanks. I need spoiling today."

Owen left, pulling a face at Shakti who grinned knowing the boss was in no mood for small talk. Cyril approached Owen's desk. It still contained the rectangular name card *DS Owen.* Cyril removed a pen from his pocket, crossed out the '*S*' before adding a letter '*I*' above. Amongst the many piles of papers was a mug. It was nibbled and chipped around the rim. In red lettering, not too dissimilar to dripping blood, was posed the question – *Is it Friday Yet?* Cyril let two fingers dip into the contents for the small wrapped sweet, an *Uncle Joe's Mint Ball*, hoping some would be lurking amongst the many empty wrappers. His rummage located the last one. Thwarted, yet again, and now feeling guilty, he placed it in the middle of Owen's desk and moved to his office.

Within minutes he had settled. Here was a total contrast to the desk he had just left. Everything had a place; nothing was out of line. There was order and symmetry.

Approaching his desk, he allowed his fingers to run over the tops of the bookcase and filing cabinets to check for dust. They were spotless. Owen appeared, his huge frame blocking the light from the open door. The cup rattled in the saucer as he entered the office.

"Is that cup drowning in its saucer, Owen? I can distinctly hear it sending out a morse code SOS."

"Sir, a moment and it will be rescued."

The rattling stopped as he carefully positioned the coffee on the mat by Cyril's *In* tray. In his other hand was his own *Harrogate Festivals* mug filled to the brim. Drips had cascaded down the side of the mug and continued in a vertical path onto his trouser leg before running onto his shoe. It was ever thus.

Cyril pointed to the stains. Owen let his eyes follow the finger and more coffee spilled onto the carpet. Cyril quickly realised nothing was going to go well that day. Glancing at the notes attached to the side of his computer screen, he noticed one was from April Richmond. April had been fast tracked up the promotional ladder as diversity was considered desirable and therefore had quickly been built into the management structure of the force. The policy had its critics as well as causing contention within the ranks. To some, it seemed totally unfair. However, April had proved herself to be capable of fulfilling her role and in a short time she had gained a great deal of respect, particularly from Owen. From the whispers on the grapevine, Cyril knew she would not be with them much longer.

"I spoke with April this morning. Bit of an unusual one, death that is, sir. Pensioner found slumped near Christ Church, High Harrogate."

Cyril frowned and sipped his coffee whilst holding a paper tissue he had taken from the box and placing it beneath the cup. He then laid another one on the puddled saucer. "Male or female and what do we know?"

"Male," Owen responded, "a Dr John Rigby, not a medical doctor, an academic, education, something to do with interpretation of language linked with science. Went above my head what she said."

Cyril's face was beginning to reflect his impatience and his lack of action spoke louder than any words, making Owen shuffle uncomfortably.

"Found at about five in the afternoon. Looked as though he was resting his eyes. Bolt upright according to April. It was only when someone went to sit on the bench near him did Rigby keel over. Must have frightened the poor bugger witless. It would me."

Cyril looked up at Owen and considering his size wondered if anything human or otherwise could possibly bring a flicker of fear to the man's stomach. "And are we suspecting anything but natural causes?"

"According to the preliminary report it could well be the heart. No other external injuries and nothing to make us believe it was foul play. His valuables were still with him."

"Next of kin?" Cyril finished the last of his coffee. "I take it those simple tasks are all dotted and crossed?"

"One son, lives in Grewelthorpe. He's a teacher and he's been notified. Wife, but they've been divorced for a number of years. April has more information. Worst of all, sir, she also has a copper's nag."

Cyril smiled. April was a natural copper and she had a copper's intuition. He knew she would not rest until the nag had been answered. "What about your investigation?"

The police had picked up concerns on a number of neighbourhood social media forums with what was believed to be drug movement. County lines. Strangely, they detailed two cars and a hooded youth who had been spotted on a number of occasions trespassing on private land.

"According to reports, sir, he's been seen mostly on the railway siding. We're presuming that a drugs' package is thrown out of the trains at strategic places for collection and then distribution." Owen slurped more coffee. "We had one witness suggest that a car dropped off the youth."

"I take it we know the make of the car and the locations?" Cyril's tone reflected his impatience.

"Sir, yes. One possible offending vehicle has been stopped and searched but nothing was found. It seems the cars drop them off but don't collect the packages. They're transported in some other way. That way there's no drug trace in the vehicle. It's also believed we're talking about distribution of tablets, probably Ecstasy, Mollies. Easily moved and concealed. In tablet form they're sold in the small plastic bags. They're found discarded all over the place, a bit like the small gas cylinders you see littering the streets. Many are in park areas and close to schools. It's an ever-increasing youth crime."

"Kids?" Cyril rested his chin on his hands and immediately thought of the child in the pram.

"As young as eleven according to reports. The attraction of the cash and maybe a new mobile phone or a pair of fashionable trainers can be marvellous motivators. Times are changing, sir."

Cyril looked towards his colleague. "How bloody true."

17

"Been on a train recently, Owen?" Cyril's face turned to look up at his colleague.

"Can't say that I have. Why?"

"They're now almost hermetically sealed once they're on the go. Even if they have windows, they're designed to prevent items from being sucked out when another train passes at speed. The drug packages can't come from a moving train. You know that, of course." He looked back down at April's note.

Owen flushed slightly before changing the subject.

"Have you taken *Liberty* home?" Owen enquired about the small bronze statue he had bought as a wedding gift and presented from the team.

"Only briefly, Owen. Julie would like it to remain here on my desk. It will return. Did you know it's of Moses holding the Decalogue and not as you thought, *Liberty*. Did a bit of digging. Once a copper, Owen, as the saying goes."

"Decalogue?" Owen's face contorted before he tilted his head back and finished his coffee. He wiped his mouth on his sleeve. "Thought Moses had a basket and ten commandments."

"Decalogue is the Ten Comma ... never mind. You have work to do?"

Owen looked into his mug, smiled and moved to the door. "That's even better then, sir. Moses led his people to the promised land. Let's hope you can do the same for us all here. I could do with a week in Scarborough. The land of milk and honey."

"You might like the milk, Owen, but not too sure about the honey. We've been there in the past!"

"Thanks for the reminder." He left swiftly.

Chapter Three

The sheeted body of Dr John Rigby lay on the post-mortem extraction table. Julie finished the autopsy and moved away. Hannah took more photographs before signalling she too was finished. Julie studied the notes – she had dictated her findings during the autopsy process and only afterwards jotted key notes on to a whiteboard. They were findings that did not seem to correlate with the cause of death, question marks needing further thought before answers would be found. This action was not in any way unusual, it was a habit she had developed over time and only when answers were found, did she wipe the board clean.

It was clear to her that Rigby had suffered from a cardiac infarction and according to his medical records he had shown evidence of previous heart related problems, nothing serious, but his medical notes had identified atrial fibrillation discovered when he was in his fifties. This, however, was in no way uncommon. Five years previously he had suffered congestive heart failure that had necessitated early retirement. Sudden, unexpected deaths were not uncommon in such cases particularly when considering the age of the patient. An acute coronary event can be witnessed in people who have no previous clinical diagnosis. Contracting a viral infection, a change in personal lifestyle or even an increase in stress level could have brought on a sudden deterioration and weakening of the heart muscle; that linked with exertion might well have contributed to the attack. Glancing again as the body was being covered, the contradiction was that for a man of his age, he showed all the signs of someone who took care of his diet and his physical wellbeing. She had seen, on closer examination of the heart, some enlargement as well as thickening to the arteries but nothing that would cause concern to him or to his GP. It was noted that his prescribed drugs should have balanced the medical condition but there was still evidence of oedema, the swelling to the legs, ankles and stomach. There was also a note detailing a recent tooth extraction, an upper left molar, as well as clear inflammation of the upper palate caused, it was thought, by a rubbing denture and some ulceration. She placed the top on the whiteboard pen and rested it on the shelf beneath before checking through his history of medication. A number of heart medicines had been prescribed. Checking the dates, many were taken during the earlier stages of diagnosis. These, she noted, had been reduced as his heart condition stabilised. It was the correct treatment. It was evident also that he had still been taking apixaban to help prevent blood clotting and stroke as well as a daily dose of digoxin.

A sample of his stomach contents had been sent for analysis. Julie had tagged a particular query owing to the excess undigested food within the stomach. She had also requested tests on bloods, ocular fluid, bile, urine and a liver sample. Toxicology would find traces of anything that should not be present and support the medical record detailing the long-term use of the specific prescribed medication.

***

Cyril felt the vibration of his mobile phone before he heard the ring. Recognising that no number was showing, he assumed it to be Julie.

"How are you?" Her voice was calm.

"I'm fine, tired but fine. Thanks for asking. Anything on the driver?" Cyril's tone failed to mask his urgency.

"Caner's workload, Cyril. I told you this morning. It's on his afternoon list. I've just examined a Dr John Rigby. Acute coronary event, Cyril. Sudden death. Did anyone witness it or try to help? There's nothing in my notes to suggest anyone did."

"No. Found by some poor sod who sat on the same bench and Rigby just keeled over. The chap said he thought he was asleep and tried shaking him gently. He then called the emergency services. The attending doctor at the scene thought he'd been dead for less than an hour." He paused. "You don't have those notes?" Cyril quizzed, uncertain as to why she would not. He heard what he thought were sheets of paper being shuffled.

"Sorry, yes. It's here. Just wanted to chat to you. If we get anything from the lab, I'll let you know. There are some question marks, more than I would have hoped for generally at this stage and until we hear to the contrary, it all appears relatively straightforward." She quickly moved on. "If I hear from Isaac, I'll get him to call you."

"Joy! Thanks. You really know how to make a man's day."

"And Cyril."

"I know, I know." He hung up. However, her uncertainty with the general diagnosis did not sit comfortably.

***

The body hung over the bridge's parapet, arms folded beneath his chest forming a cushion against the cold stone. A grey hood concealed any distinguishing features of his head and face. He was like a bird of prey waiting. Occasionally, he lifted one leg before gently shaking the foot and returning it slowly to the ground. The youth concentrated on the twin railway lines that ran beneath. To either side of the track the shrubs and trees formed a wild, dense border. There was only one pavement running across the Langcliffe Avenue Bridge. He turned and looked along the tracks in the opposite direction towards Harrogate town centre. A similar bridge spanned St James' Drive a couple of hundred yards along the track. Here the vegetation had been severely denuded along either side, exposing most of the track area to both houses and roads running close by. There was neither privacy nor concealment. Here, below where he roosted, however, was the entrance spur to the old Brunswick Tunnel. Almost invisible from this view point as it was wrapped in trees, it offered the perfect place to access the track.

Removing his phone, he checked the app. The Bluetooth link showed the package to be about twenty metres to the right of the rails, although from his position it was not visible. Putting the phone away, he slipped a finger onto the cuff of his sleeve dragging it over to reveal his watch. There was obviously a delay and his heart fluttered. He needed the train to pass and then the line would be clear. Turning again, he checked Langcliffe Avenue. Apart from a pedestrian walking in his direction there was nothing.

It seemed too quiet. His nerves grew as the seconds ticked by.

In moments, and for no apparent reason, he seemed to sense the train's approach before he heard it. The two vibrations from his phone's alarm against his thigh confirmed the time the train should leave Hornbeam Station. Looking down the line to the curve in the track, he let his eyes focus on one spot. Slowly the front of the York-Harrogate train burst around the corner. Its twin-tone horn pierced the silence with an intimidating, shrill cry, scattering pigeons to flight yet having the opposite effect on the watcher who leaned over the stone wall even further. The pedestrian, now almost alongside, paused as her attention was drawn to the watching youth and the approaching train. *The Railway Children* came into her head and made her innocently and instinctively raise a hand to wave at the train, only to be suddenly pushed to one side as the youth left his perch and ran past her. Regaining her balance, she mumbled under her breath before continuing. The train was now disappearing towards the town centre. There would not be another for forty minutes. The track would be clear.

Within seconds the youth turned and entered a private garden. Sticking to the side of the hedge, he soon followed the natural contours of the land. Here the trees were close as he headed towards the south portal of the Brunswick Tunnel. It was not his first visit and he hoped it would not be his last; it was a lucrative collection for little effort and limited risk. Climbing the low wall, he began to descend through brambles, nettles and low-slung branches that made movement both difficult and noisy. Once at the bottom, the water and mud conspired against his progress.

He knew, however, there was no need to hurry. The parcel would be there, it was going nowhere without him. His phone told him so.

**

Owen took the call at 11.37. A home owner living on Langcliffe Avenue had called 101 having seen a youth on her property. It was reported he had entered the garden and climbed the stone boundary wall at the far end directly above the banking to the Brunswick Tunnel portal, an area that was once a spur from the main railway line that ran into Harrogate. The tunnel, built in 1862, had brought steam trains into the heart of Harrogate beneath The Stray, to keep the trains from polluting the town. The four hundred yard tunnel was soon made obsolete after the construction of a main station but it remained. To Owen, the thought of it brought back memories of a previous case. A crime of cruel deeds had taken place within and Owen paused in reflection. "Like the gate to hell," he mumbled to himself. Consequently, this remaining portal had been securely closed with reinforced grilles that were designed to allow nothing but bats to enter and bats and water to leave. There was, however, still the 'V' shaped cutting running from the end of the private garden towards the track. For those determined and bold enough, access to the cutting and to the line was easy.

The attending officer had noted the security camera positioned to the rear of the house and the subsequent footage had been forwarded. Owen watched the grainy CCTV images and although little could be gleaned, they had at least some supporting form of identification on which to act. He ordered still images to be enhanced and posted on the North Yorkshire website and social media pages in the hope someone might identify the youth. He also requested CCTV footage from the morning trains and the stations to either side of the bridge. He held little hope. He thought of Cyril's words, *hermetically sealed.* Could the items collected come from the bridge? *It is unlikely to be found by anyone other than someone who knows it is there on the edge of the railway lines.* He smiled. *A whole new meaning to the term County Lines,* he thought.

County Line groups were well-prepared. Discovering their leaders and operatives had in the past proven to be akin to the street and fairground game, *Find the Lady,* but without the three pots and the pea. To many forces, they were becoming will-o'-the-wisps. Looking down he saw the solitary mint ball on his desk. It was the one bright spot of his morning.

Chapter Four

Dr John Rigby's son played with his phone. His finger flicked the screen as if reading social media posts as he waited in the entrance hall of Harrogate police station. From each ear, white pods protruded and his head moved more slowly to the music than his tapping foot. His movements seemed unnatural, more born from nervousness and anxiety than musical rhythm. For a large building, the Reception area was simply that. Painted blue, it seemed cold and clinical and no amount of ringing phones and chattering voices from those working behind the desk counter removed this austerity. A counter ran down most of one wall towards the outside doors. Staring around he saw little else apart from a large noticeboard. He took little interest. Other doors remained closed and somewhat mysterious apart from one with a small oval window sitting central and two thirds up from the floor. It was skinned in what appeared to be metal sheeting but painted the same colour as the rest.

He was early, but for some strange reason felt anxious. Maybe it was the clinical feel to his immediate surroundings that set him on edge or the room before him he assumed to be a holding cell. He also had the uncomfortable feeling that his father's death might not have been as straightforward as first believed.

He had identified the body soon afterwards and

considering his father's health record, his death was not unexpected and, on first hearing the news, seemed natural. The call from the police, however, had placed a seed of doubt in his mind that his initial assumption was premature. He focused on the music. In his peripheral vision he noticed the door opening to his right, immediately drawing his attention. Turning to look, he saw a large gentleman. His tie was skewed to one side and the left side collar of his shirt pointed skywards.

"Mr Rigby?" Owen moved quickly and thrust out his hand. "Detective Inspector Owen. Thanks for coming. Sorry if you've had …"

Ian Rigby had removed his ear pods and immediately interrupted. "I was early, Detective Inspector, no need to apologise."

The teacher in Rigby wanted to straighten the man's collar but he resisted.

"Please come this way." Owen swiped his pass over the key pad and pushed, opening the door whilst allowing the key card to swing on the lanyard.

***

The atmosphere in the greenhouse was sultry and although the day started cool, it had improved bringing sunshine and warmth. The vine tomatoes strung along one side were well past their best. The leaves had clearly given up first and become edged in russet and ochre, but the vines still contained the last of the fruit even if they exhibited a reluctance to ripen. They contrasted with the pot plants that filled another section. They were a rich mix of greens and seemed far more exotic.

Fried green tomatoes at the whistle stop café, came to mind as fingers busied in bringing some semblance of order to the place. Even the untrained eye could see that it clearly needed more than a tidy. The structure was showing definite signs of age. Some of the glazing units were cracked while the majority had weathered towards dirt-skinned opacity. The timber was also clearly rotten in places but it would have to do. It had served its purpose for another season and it would not be long before it received its annual clean and disinfection, but more had to be done before that … much more. Taking a moment to pause, there was still the familiar aroma in the air that can only come from the tomato plant.

To the other side of the greenhouse were the exotics, some trimmed plants and herbs set in pots along the right-hand shelves. The leaves here were rich and glossy. "My three Graces, Pereskia bleo, Cinacanthus nutans and Vitex trifolia. You never seem to lose your depth of colour, do you?" A hand touched each plant as if caressing it.

The half-full trug was placed on the small outer wall before removing the cast iron weight in the shape of a lion, a souvenir acquired during college days, thus allowing the door to be closed. As usual it stuck momentarily against the door jamb but a sharp tug, a technique used over many years, brought the door to a close along with the accompanying rattle of some of the many loose panes. It was always a worrying moment, as if the structure were about to collapse.

How many years have I been cultivating here? The inner thoughts were like whispered words, lost to the breeze, as the trug was collected and tired steps moved away and towards the cottage. It had been a wilderness that first year, an overgrown jungle of a mess. Now after all that work established shrubs and trees filled the garden throughout the seasons with myriad colours and scents. On either side of the pathway, the herbaceous border grew compact and tall. The glory days when it had first been tamed and a new order given to its structure had faded as time did not allow the work needed. With the approaching autumn many of the plants were dying back but it still held a beauty that was once so common in the English garden. The butterflies and the bees liked it too. This was not a show garden, it had been allowed to spread and intermingle bringing a softness and freedom of pure, inseparable, botanical entanglement.

The sound of a wagon's horn, thunderously loud and annoying, broke the silence. Birds burst overhead all flapping wings and wild calls before skimming low over the trees at the far edge of the garden. Sometimes, when walking barefoot, the traffic's vibration could be felt through the ground as more building continued within the village. Today seemed better, there was none and besides, it was too late in the day to be shoeless.

The kitchen seemed cold after the hour spent in the greenhouse. Two trays sat on the highly polished oak table. One contained a part-finished jigsaw, the other the necessary pieces to complete it. There was a clear strategy to the way in which the pieces had been sorted, not by shape but by colour. After a moment's pause, and a degree of concentration, three more pieces were put in position before the kettle was filled. Cuttings from the trug were placed into a small pan of water waiting on the stove. A gentle heat was selected and the overhead extractor switched to low. Set too high, the screaming drone from the fan would be annoying.

Cupping the mug of steaming coffee seemed to be a catalyst for reflection. The small dog was asleep, curled into a tight ball. Strangely, the nagging pain seemed to have grown less intense but it was still there, a constant throb that pulsed and quelled enthusiasm for anything other than thought and reflection. Drive, commitment and ambition had slowly been eroded since the diagnosis had been confirmed. It had been replaced by a cloudy darkness filled by inner demons. There was no fear now; anger and resentment had replaced it, spreading like the disease itself. In some ways, the resentment had brought more than a degree of resilience as well as a growing satisfaction.

Why me? Why now? Seemed repetitive questions that were probably normal vocabulary to anyone receiving a severe diagnosis and were rhetorically asked daily. This was usually performed when facing the mirror first thing in the morning and last thing in the evening but like all rhetorical questions, they were never answered. They floated in the constant void that had been allowed to fill with resentment and maybe that was God's will, or much more likely, it was Satan's curse.

This room, like all rooms in the house, was once immaculate but now, like the greenhouse and the garden, it was a shadow of its former self. Leaning over, another piece of the jigsaw was tried, lifted, manoeuvred before accepting defeat and returned to the second tray. As the coffee came to parted lips the deeper, soulful thoughts began to appear amidst the brain fog. Slowly they came to the fore:

You work all of your life in a caring profession in the hope of securing a retirement that is both rewarding and full. You care for people throughout life, within personal relationships and whilst at work. You do your best, try to put people first. It's like, as my father always used to say, life's bank. You deposit kindness to save for a rainy day. With relationships come memories and memories, he always said, were made so that we can have roses in December.

A laugh broke the thought pattern, a cynical laugh, a sceptic utterance, the type of laugh that was now much more common than ever before. For the first time for many years there were feelings of strong resentment and bitterness.

You can buy bloody roses all year round. We don't need memories for that but we do need to remember. We need to recall the good times and not to forget the bad; those who have supported us throughout life and those who have pulled the rug from beneath us, those who have set obstacles in our way or tried to make us do what we know to be wrong for their own gain. Those purporting to be our friend and colleague, to have our best interest at heart, only then to use and abuse you, then bury you with a stick of chalk as thanks for the years of toil within the world of teaching.

Is this festering disease I find I am burdened with, a penance for some wrong-doing in my past? Is it a hair shirt I must now wear to my grave? Or is it a friend, an amulet to guide me on the path I must take, a path less trodden? Whatever it is, I feel it's the devil's curse and with it, I just feel more and more resentful.

31

Spotting a likely piece of the jigsaw interrupted the thought pattern. Leaning over, a hand left the mug and selected it. The image appeared to be part of red blossom. As the hand hovered confidently over the gap the piece slipped straight in. The bubbling water from the pan rattled the lid allowing splashes of water to fall onto the cooker. The fizzing and crackling interrupted the moment of satisfaction.

***

Rigby's son could hold back no longer. As the interview progressed, he chose his time to point to his own collar and then to Owen's. Owen took the hint and finally adjusted his appearance.

"Been a busy day, Mr Rigby. Thank you. Now, where was I?"

"You asked about our last meeting. Me and my father."

Owen raised a finger. "Yes, thanks. Go on. You and your father."

"We try to meet regularly. Since mum went, we used to meet up for a beer. He also needed reassurance about his health. The one bright spot was joining the internet group of ex-colleagues. It seemed to lift his general mood."

"Tell me a little more about this group."

"I helped him get to grips with Facebook. As you can imagine technology is a little like magic to him. I noticed a few familiar names when he first started. You need to understand that I did most of the typing during those initial interactions but he seems, sorry, seemed to have mastered it. He never asked for any more help, at least."

"Familiar names. Mr Rigby?"

"I only recognised some names but I knew Stan Cooper

fairly well. He'd been to the house as I was growing up. In fact, Inspector, he was quite a guiding influence when I decided to follow my father into the profession. He was the one who encouraged me which was refreshing as many of our friends, family and his colleagues tried to dissuade me from my chosen career path. My father was one of those can you believe?"

Owen continued to make notes. "Can you recall any of the names and what about this Facebook page? I take it it's a private group?"

"Barbara Burton was the administrator, the gate guardian. Very strict about who was allowed to penetrate the walls." He chuckled. "Very authoritarian. There was a Joan, that was an easy name to remember but the surname I can't recall. Thought it might be my mother but there was no second person added as a friend with the name Rigby. It was just referenced in the text occasionally. A Pauline Shirley, I remember her from being a kid because of her surname and a Seex as that always either made me blush or giggle. There was an Evans, and a Masters. Her first name might be Michelle but I couldn't be sure. Greg Lewis, and a Norma but surname I couldn't say. Funnily enough, I tried to look into the site but admin was rather tight. I believe it was by personal invitation only. It was funny seeing some of the names as they took me back to my youth."

"Why did your father retire, Mr Rigby?"

***

Taking the pan from the stove the lid was lifted gingerly. The hot liquid had turned a dirty brown-green colour not too dissimilar to strong tea. It was poured through a sieve into a

Pyrex bowl and placed on a shelf to cool. The jigsaw called but it would have to wait a little longer. From a bottom cupboard three small Kilner jars were removed. They were held up to the window one by one to ensure they were clean. Their lids and seals were checked. Soon the cooled liquid was poured in equal measure into each. Returning to the table a finger checked the soil in the plant pot containing the peace lily. It did not like to be too wet. It would do for another day before water was needed.

***

"Health grounds." A flush of red burst onto Rigby's cheeks and he looked down at his fingers as he spoke. "To be honest, after mum divorced him, he never seemed to be the same. Before she left, he was always at work. Late nights, weekends away with either conferences or union matters. About that time mum had the belief that he was having an affair."

"And is it your belief that he was?" Owen asked.

Rigby shrugged his shoulders. "I was too young to pay attention. I knew things weren't right, the increase in the number of arguments and the imposed silences. Funny, my mum's growing frustration and possible fear didn't seem to change him, probably strengthened his resolve to live life the way he wanted to. He could be domineering and arrogant. He was always kind to me as was Mum."

"And what about your mother?" Owen leaned back. Family trauma interested him having been brought up by his grandparents. He had known difficult times himself.

"She was a teacher too as you'll probably know. The rumours that abound within an LEA can be very debilitating and she would have had much to weather. She lost most of her enthusiasm for teaching; she was once very career focused. She went through the motions, did the bare minimum and concentrated on her garden. She rented a property temporarily until she found a house in Killinghall. After a while when she knew she could pay the bills, she then went teaching part-time and filled her days looking after me."

"When did she separate from your father?"

"Unofficially? When she confronted him. I believe someone told Mum, and from my recollection, it was a woman who had been having an affair with my father. He had moved on to someone else, someone probably younger and more naive. When she confronted him, he admitted he'd been unfaithful for a number of years and that was the final straw that broke the relationship. In some ways, Inspector Owen, Mum seemed to shed a huge burden that she'd been carrying when it all came out, the burden that comes and grows heavier when fed with suspicion, uncertainty and fear."

"And you, Mr Rigby?"

"I went with my mother. She'd been through enough and I knew I would fall out with Dad. He was a selfish sod and as I grew older, I witnessed that even more. I left Killinghall when I went to University, returned home briefly and then flew the nest when I could afford to. It was never the same after the separation but I guess it never can be."

"Not wanting to make you blush or giggle, what about Seex?" Owen smiled as he posed the question, trying to lift the mood.

"It was a name, a strange one at that. If I did meet him, I don't remember the occasion."

35

"His first name?"

Rigby shook his head. "As I said, just the name, Seex has stuck up here." He tapped the side of his head with his finger.

Chapter Five

Dr Isaac Caner popped his head around Julie's office door. His glasses were perched just above his forehead. As he had little hair other than to the sides, they were immediately noticeable and gave the appearance of an extra pair of eyes looking towards her.

"Do you have a minute?" His tone was more sombre than usual.

Closing the file she was working on, she pointed to the chair. "Sure. Problem?"

"The driver, Cyril's driver." He paused and brought down his glasses before opening a small folder. "Not a mark on him apart from the usual pressure marks from the restraining seat belt. No evidence of knocks to the head or wrist damage from the steering wheel. Usual airbag residue on exposed skin and within the ears and hair but little of significance in the eyes and none in the trachea, nasal tract nor lungs."

"He was dead before the car hit anything," Julie interrupted, having predicted his next sentence.

"Sudden death. There's historical evidence of heart failure. Hypertension at his last check and scanning his record, he received medication. According to this, he was prescribed digoxin for fibrillation. The latest ECG records show improvement."

He took the copy of the results and passed it to her

before removing his glasses and tossing them carelessly onto the desk. He sat back, steepled his fingers before resting the top of the pointed fingers beneath his chin. "I read the notes on your case, a Dr John Rigby, after I saw your scribblings on the whiteboard written after your investigation. I must try doing that myself, it's very organised. I listened to your dictation too. Will you take a look at Paul Seex? There are too many coincidences to be coincidental if that makes sense! Interesting name Seex, don't you think?"

Julie smiled. "Sex with an extra vitamin," she mumbled remembering Cyril's words.

Caner neither commented nor smiled. Standing, he grabbed his glasses and made for the door. His face still contained the puzzled expression he had displayed when he entered.

Once gowned, Caner took delight in showcasing the patient's heart. "If it were me and I was his age, I'd be happy with that. Some enlargement but within the parameters. The medication seems to have been working." He handed the organ to her. "No clear signs of a failing heart but I believe it did just that."

"As you're aware from my notes, Isaac, very similar condition to Rigby's. I'll be curious to see what comes back from toxicology."

Turning, Caner looked at her quizzically before returning the heart to the stainless steel dish with a degree of reverence.

Julie pulled off a glove. "This cause of death in men of this age is happening all the time so let's not forget that. The fact that we had these two arriving within a day of each other with what appears to be almost identical symptoms could amount to nothing." Julie tried to reassure him that their initial diagnosis was correct. "Sudden death. Both suffered from heart issues. Natural causes."

Isaac turned to her. "Let's wait as you suggest for toxicology, my dear." Caner adjusted the dish once more. "As I say, let's just wait and see."

Julie suddenly felt uncomfortable on hearing his patronising close of sentence. In all their time together, he had never called her *my dear*. He was the consummate professional. It made her want to review immediately her results. Had she missed something that Caner had spotted? If she had, then surely he would have said so or had he discovered something during his autopsy of Seex that was not present in her investigation?

***

More out of curiosity than necessity, April Richmond looked across at the bench on which John Rigby had been found. To her dismay traces of the blue and white plastic police tape could be seen to one side, littering the place. Closing the car door, she glanced at the clock on the church tower and then back towards the solitary empty bench. A typical Harrogate serpent style seat, it was sited on the grass and positioned towards the end of the graveyard looking away and across The Stray. The whole setting looked idyllic with the stone church positioned within a sea of green. It was so close to the town centre and yet seemed very isolated. *Isolated enough to commit murder?* She thought not. Something did not sit right in her mind and that was why she was there.

Collecting the tape, she swiftly wound it into a ball and as there was no litter bin, she stuffed it in her pocket. Aware there had been no Forensic investigation, she took a moment to inspect the bench. To the front was a row of flagstones. On the backrest were two small plaques, one black, the other made from what looked like brass. The weather had taken its toll on both fittings, each had been placed there in memory of a loved one. Removing her phone, she took a photograph of each. To the right, towards the very end of the wood, was some writing. It appeared to be initials and a date written in what seemed to be silver, indelible marker ink. It contrasted with the rest of the bench's appearance looking relatively fresh. There was little weathering.

UR / WYS

88

April sat briefly and jotted them down as they were written. The letters WYS were slightly below the line of the letters UR. Her immediate thoughts were of a lover's expression but then '88' would mean thirty-three years ago and the bench had certainly not been in this position for that length of time.

Names beginning with the letter 'U', probably female as they were set slightly higher, she thought: Ursula and Urania came immediately to mind but that was it. Even her knowledge of biblical names seemed to have deserted her. She resorted to the internet but considering the results, decided she was overthinking. Even the male names proved too far-fetched.

Standing, she turned and looked at the graveyard just behind the bench. Maybe the answer was in there. She stepped over the low wall. The remains of lead trapped within holes that once held metal railings were still visible. Evidence of their removal, the need for iron during the war had robbed many a wall. Most of the grand houses of Harrogate had lost their metalwork to support the war effort. April paced carefully between the grave stones looking at the names. She paused at the grave of Ashwood Longstaff. His life was short. It conjured an image of one of Robin Hood's merry men. She then looked away as she thought it more likely to be the name of his weapon. *Bring me my Ash wood long staff*, she said to herself as the tune to Jerusalem overtook her musings. She returned to her car. As the melody grew in her head, the nag began to fade.

***

Owen looked up as April approached her desk.

"You're a bit early for the night shift, Richmond," he grinned. "I believe they used to say you were quartered in the old days when you were late but then to understand that you'd have to ask Cyril." It fell on deaf ears.

"Had to go and look at the bench where Rigby was found before work. Just something nagged at me. It's hard to describe, Owen. It's like an itch and I can't rest until it's been scratched." She removed the screwed up police tape from her pocket and dropped it in the bin.

"And the itch?" Owen asked, mustering a degree of enthusiasm, believing her quest to be folly.

"False alarm ..." she mumbled whilst slipping her jacket onto the back of her chair. She offered Owen a cursory glance. "... A waste of time, I think." Her facial expression contradicted her words and Owen, noting this, quickly changed the subject.

"This will tax you. Why do we have reports of a feral youth trespassing on the railway lines if you can't throw anything from a moving train?" He paused only briefly before holding up a finger hoping to prevent her from answering. "According to Cyril, the majority of the trains on this line only allow the doors to open when stationary and yet we've had another call regarding a kid on the line by Langcliffe Avenue."

April carefully added the initials she had seen on the bench to paper and taped it to the board next to her desk. *UR/WYS 88.*

"Playing chicken?" she mumbled, her tone showing neither belief in her answer nor enthusiasm for the question.

Owen shook his head. "Please, April, just give it some thought, that's all I ask. I can see no logic."

"From what you've said recently you believe it's more than likely drugs related. Maybe the packets come from the road and not the train, from the bridge or maybe from someone working for the railway. Do the guards, or are they now called conductors?" She screwed her face in thought. "Conductors, I think. Do they have the means to open a window?" Her engaged tone camouflaged that her thoughts were still partly elsewhere.

Owen frowned. It was something to consider. In the past he had realised, that with the committing of crimes, both a casual yet swift approach was often favoured and the adage *doing it right under people's noses* seemed to be apposite. Maybe he was looking in the wrong place.

"I don't know. Thanks, April. You always seem to be able to come up with another angle. I'll be damned, these dealers are like will-o'-the-wisps," he mumbled to himself but his words carried over to April.

She looked over her computer screen. "Interesting phenomenon. Folk tales abound."

Owen frowned and scratched his head. "What phenomenon?"

"Will-o'-the-wisps. Made up like Jenny Greenteeth and Peg Powler."

"My gran used to tell me about Jenny Greenteeth to keep me away from ponds, the canal and the like. Scared the shit out of me she did. I can still see her screwed up face inches from mine putting on this evil voice. 'I'm Jenny Greenteeth and I'll drown you.' The strange thing was, April, she'd no teeth in, they were kept in a glass for best so it contradicted the whole idea. Scary as hell though!"

April laughed out loud. "Ignis fatuus is the Latin term meaning foolish fire. They are mysterious lights which hover in dark places. The wisps lead travellers and the unwary astray so you're more accurate than you think. Your gangs lead youngsters astray and probably the flashing of torch light or car headlights is their siren's call."

"Learn something with you every day, April. Tends to be useless information that I'll never need again but you're generous with your general knowledge. Ignis fartous. I'll remember that, use it as my trump card in the pub quiz!" He winked.

April shook her head and was about to correct him but realised he was teasing and thought better of it. Giving out an audible sigh, she lowered her face behind the computer screen. It was like casting pearls before swine.

Chapter Six

The telephone in the hallway rang. The shrill tone seemed to hang in the semi-darkness until the answerphone intercepted the call.

"Gadding about again?" The caller's voice was shrill and confident, displaying a degree of resignation that she would be talking to a machine again before stating the obvious. "I'm talking to a bloody answer machine yet again. It's Norma. Have you heard the tragic news? First it was Paul Seex and then Dr John, you know, John Rigby. I had a drink with Paul on Saturday in town and he seemed fine. Only a coffee mind. Well he moaned about his ticker and said he had a bit of a cold but nothing untoward and now he's gone. Dreadful accident. Killed a young mother before his car ploughed into some railings. He probably shouldn't have been driving but you know what men are like for ignoring advice." She paused again. "I hate talking to this bloody machine. Both dead and gone! He looked the picture of health too. You just never know. Ring me back when you can. I'll try and find out more about what happened to John. I have his wife's number somewhere. She left him years ago if you remember, bit of a Lothario by all accounts. You might remember her. She came to some of our earlier meetings but then just stopped attending. You'd know her if you saw her, I'm sure of that. I suppose we'll be attending two funerals shortly but sadly no weddings. I do love a good wedding." Her manner suddenly seemed quite callous as if the two deaths had interrupted future plans.

The voice had been resoundingly clear even at the far end of the passageway as Melanie Masters came from the kitchen. Norma's strident voice had echoed around the tiled floored passageway. The red light on the telephone now blinked once. Melanie dried her hands on her apron as she approached the phone. Pressing one of the buttons, she was informed that the message had been deleted. Melanie had heard about Seex but she had been surprised how quickly Rigby's death had been reported. The private internet group had been alive with speculation after Seex's death. With two in quick succession, they would not be able to contain themselves.

The Facebook group comprised mainly ex-teachers from the North Yorkshire Education Authority. Many, as they often liked to pronounce, had dedicated their working years to toiling at the *chalkface.* Over time, some had been promoted to different levels within the education system. Norma, like Seex, had become an advisor, whereas Rigby had been far more adventurous and moved authority to climb the promotional ladder. He returned to take up a post as a senior science advisor to then find himself Deputy Director of Education. He held these positions for a number of years from the mid to late eighties until, like many of his era, retiring. It had to be said that one or two soon found they were not ready for retirement, especially those who left early with enhanced pensions, and were prepared to dabble in a bit of lecturing, supply teaching or home tutoring. To those still working, it seemed like pure avarice. The majority shared their memories on the group website. Old photographs and 'do you remember' comments were a daily occurrence on the site. As time passed there seemed to be greater enthusiasm for meetings and gatherings. Nostalgia seemed to burn more strongly. It had been at one of these reunions that Norma and Melanie had become friends for the second time around, sharing their memories in an artificial, glossy warmth that mutual reflection on past times often brings.

Melanie had no difficulty in remembering the first time she had met Dr John Rigby. On that occasion, as she recalled, he had been neither a Doctor nor a gentleman. It occurred during a science teachers' course at Harrogate's Teachers' Centre, housed in the upstairs rooms of the primary school on Belford Road. Her mind moved away from Rigby as she closed her eyes and visualised the place. It brought a shudder as she recalled how the upper rooms always seemed so cold. It was suggested that the place was haunted as the conveniently located site in Harrogate town centre was once a hospital and later known as the Harrogate Infirmary. Returning to the incident proper, she thought it was probably towards the end of 1979 or early 1980. It was definitely winter; she immediately recalled the black leather boots she had bought. It was a course designed to promote the teaching of science through a thematic approach to be linked to both primary and secondary schools. To many there, it was yet again a dilution of educational content and a nod to the fashionable, airy-fairy approach that seemed to lack rigor and focus. It had been driven by the philosophy of equality. It would allow the less academic students to enjoy science and

47

chemistry, an argument that to many dedicated teachers of the subject seemed both facile and insulting, but then, professional judgement could not hold a candle to trends.

The tutor was some whiz kid who had enthused throughout the course, peppering his lecture with the annoying repetition of the word 'issues'.

"Not working this approach, your students would face issues and many might find issues within issues."

Melanie remembered wanting to call out 'Bless you!' on each occasion but managed to resist even though the word sounded more like a sneeze than a key word. If she were honest, she believed he was making it up as he went along. He never fully told the group what any of the issues were, only they would be faced in abundance. To Melanie, he had clearly been promoted beyond his capabilities.

In those halcyon days there was funding for such learning and it was a bonus to be released from school for a time under the title of *professional development*. If you took it seriously, then it might be construed as just that. To some, it was a morning or a day out of the classroom, time with colleagues away from the kids, a bit of a laugh and a free lunch, the opportunity to catch up and share tales of the classroom.

It had been late in the afternoon during some practical activity, role play, they called it, when Rigby slipped his hand on her leg and allowed it to move along her thigh. At first, believing it to be accidental, she said nothing but his true intentions soon became clear. It brought a chuckle to her throat as she recalled the faces of those teachers in the room as she let out a shriek. Rigby's reddening face was witnessed by many but only she saw the venom in his eyes.

Melanie moved to the stairs and perched on the second step before turning her gaze to admire the coloured, patterned, leaded glass that filled the vestibule door and frame. She laughed to herself remembering his face as clearly as if it were yesterday. She had given him a few choice words in a way that those sitting near their table could clearly hear and understand what had taken place. He had immediately apologised and had protested his innocence too strongly, as if the hand had found its way there and moved towards the hem of her skirt in error. She remembered the deep, red flush filling his face and neck. It was, however, his eyes and the pure look of hatred she recalled seeing. From that moment on, there had been an armed truce between them whenever they met. If she were honest, she had forgotten about him and the incident until years later and the beginning of a new term when their professional relationship deteriorated even more. In the cold light of the hallway she could not recall the year. She remembered with great clarity his return, not as many teachers did, to take up a position within a classroom or as a deputy headteacher, but to be appointed to the post of a senior member of the advisory team within the Authority, a position of power. On reflection, it should not have surprised her. Back then, it seemed to her and to so many of her female colleagues, being male and having a reputation as a bit of a Lothario was one of the unwritten qualities men needed to acquire to gain a further footing on the promotional ladder. This ladder, more often than not at that time, was controlled by similar fellows tarred with the same brush. It was simple, for many to gain promotion one had to climb the slippery, promotional pole – a female reference to the male organ.

It was, to those who cared to look, a boys' network. She felt the frustration bubble as it had done so often in the past. It was the feeling of impotence. Now they call it the glass ceiling, but then it was a concrete slab that kept females in their place unless of course ... She shuddered at the thought. Thankfully, as the years passed, times quickly changed for the better.

Stealthily, her cat had crept down the stairs and she felt the push of his face begin to lever a gap between her body and arm. His warmth was immediate, his determination focused before finally he achieved his goal and settled on her lap. His tail, forever dancing, caressed her face.

"You boys are all the same," she whispered, whilst stroking the side of his head. "You can get where dirt can't. You're determined to get what you want when you want it. It's a good job we girls let you, and it's a good job I love you."

The cat gently clawed at her loose apron and gave out a contented purr.

"The boys' network," she repeated. "We're all men together." She mimicked the words. She had heard them said to a male candidate who had been appointed over her in an interview for promotion, as he was led from the waiting room. Promotional chances for women were clearly hamstrung, unless of course, you played their game or you were emotionally attached to one ... "Bastards!" The word resonated with the venom she expelled and it seemed to bounce from the walls. The cat sensed it too, slipped from her lap and through the balustrade, before making its way to the kitchen.

Chapter Seven

Cyril had received the call from Julie fifty minutes earlier. She needed to see him and she had a brief window of opportunity if he could get over to her office, insisting that a discussion over the phone would not be ethical.

He arrived early and was shown to her office. It was always a place he entered with a degree of trepidation as his curiosity for the unusual objects displayed outweighed his ability to stomach the explanation. The various specimen jars sitting on the shelves never seemed to be as they were described on the labels. They were parts of people, real people. Usually, these parts are hidden either within the body or behind clothing so seeing the pickled penis on a lower shelf on his previous visit had been the last straw. It had become his bête noire and he found it difficult to maintain his focus away from the jar. It seemed to draw him as if testing his resolve. It brought a shudder across his shoulders. Moving to the left of Julie's desk, he found a smaller container, one he could not recall seeing before. Lifting it, he could not fail to observe it left a clear circle, highlighting the thin coating of dust that covered the shelf. He ran his finger along leaving a definite line only to be immediately startled.

"Do I come into your office and root through your drawers?" Julie's angry words were clearly simulated.

"Needs a bloody good dust." He held up the jar whilst

moving towards her. "What is it?"

"It's a double appendix, Cyril. In addition to a normal appendix arising from the caecum at the usual site, there was a second appendix arising from the caecum along the lines of the taenia about three centimetres away from the first." She paused aware of the confusion on his face. "Let's just say it's uncommon. It's a specimen I like to show colleagues at lectures. Now put it back and don't drop it."

He located the exact spot and replaced the specimen jar on the dust-free circle. "We don't need it, our appendix, I believe, so having two? Wouldn't it be better if they were removed at birth?"

Julie raised her eyes and tutted.

"Wrong. A little knowledge, Cyril, is a dangerous thing, particularly in the mind of a detective. You should know that the appendix is designed to protect good bacteria in the gut. That way, when the gut is affected by a bout of diarrhoea or other illness that cleans out the intestines, the good bacteria in the appendix can repopulate the digestive system and keep you healthy." Her speech was almost monotone.

"Right. That's why it's recommended to eat a live yoghurt whilst taking antibiotics?" Cyril responded, a look of one-upmanship on his face.

Julie did not reply but rolled her eyes knowing he would always try to have the last word.

Now feeling more confident, he continued. "I once read that lighthouse keepers had to have their appendix removed before they were allowed to be isolated on one of the lights. Apochryphal or true?"

Julie maintained her silence whilst slipping behind her

desk. "Much as I'd love to chat about things past, my key words when I rang were that *I had a brief window of opportunity*. Brief is key and it's things present I wanted to discuss not lighthouses and what's in the jars, Cyril."

"Yes, sorry. Got carried away."

"A bit like your two dead septuagenarian pedagogues." She looked up at Cyril whose return frown encouraged her to continue. "Seex and Rigby. I had a chat with Isaac and we believe there are a number of significant similarities linked to their deaths. We have therefore intensified our examination of the samples taken, particularly those sent to toxicology."

Cyril leaned forward. Suddenly his enthusiasm had become focused. "How similar?"

"We're guessing, but it's professional guesswork, I add. We feel their medical conditions had been exacerbated in some way. External forces. I'm sure the police files will be full of such cases where the perpetrator knows of the victim's medical weaknesses and acts upon them, either to kill immediately, or over a longer period of time. We know that they were acquainted both professionally and socially for a number of years. They both worked within the same field and for the same LEA." Julie paused and looked at Cyril. "Local education authority, this authority. Both retired some time ago, both early and neither by choice. These two were finished on medical grounds according to their histories."

"So, what do you think killed them, Julie?"

Julie tapped the top of her desk with her finger. "If I were to hazard a guess right now it would be some kind of toxic substance."

"Toxic? Chemicals?" Cyril's question was now keen and direct. "Killed?" He paused and frowned, putting his thoughts into context. "Murdered? Or suicide?"

"What do you tell your people, Cyril? *Keep an open mind* and that's what I'll be doing until all the results are back in. As you know, toxic can mean the overindulgence of a substance or substances to the point where it's detrimental to the person's health. If you consumed enough toothpaste it would kill you. In your case, Black Sheep ale!" Her comment was swiftly followed by her hand slipping onto his and it lightened the moment. "Kidding! Now speaking of toothpaste, Rigby had this in his jacket pocket." She took out a small bottle from the left-hand drawer. "If it's what it says on the damaged label, and we'll know those facts soon, it's a treatment for gum irritation caused through ill-fitting dentures or gum blistering. It was clear that he'd had a tooth extraction some days prior to his death and the cavity area was red and inflamed. I'm of the opinion it was used to calm that. It's a local anaesthetic and antiseptic tincture."

Cyril picked up the bottle and turned it in his fingers.

"But what I wanted you to know is that this case might not be as simple as we first thought. It may be worth your looking into their backgrounds. You might just then be at the head of the game and as soon as we have something, we'll get the facts to you. Remember, at this stage, it's just our strong, professional hunch. Cyril, they may well have been poisoned but that's strictly off the record."

A moment's silence followed as Cyril's eyes inadvertently returned to the jar containing the pickled penis.

"I'll wrap that as a birthday present if you're not careful, my man! Did you hear what I said?"

"Poisoned. Off the record. Thank you. That's a great help."

"And by the way, when NASA was planning the Apollo space programme, they considered the possibility of appendicitis but decided buying time with antibiotics was better than a prophylactic appendectomy."

"No antibiotics for the lighthouse keepers, of course. Medical science!" Cyril riposted.

"It will be developments in Forensic medicine that will allow us to find out more about your dead couple and confirm my belief."

***

Mrs Carrie Wilkinson had called at the station and was seated and waiting in the entrance as Owen made his way down from his work area. Pressing the door release he moved towards the front desk. On hearing the door Carrie looked up, but only briefly. Her eyes returned to stare at the grey flooring as she continued to wring her hands nervously.

Owen listened to the duty officer. "She saw a youth on Langcliffe Avenue Bridge. Time corresponds to the call from the home owner. She's unsure and doesn't want to waste police time. Nervous, like. Here are her details. Name's Carrie Wilkinson. Mrs."

Owen nodded to the duty officer, turned and moved towards her. "Mrs Wilkinson?" His voice was reassuring. She looked up. "Detective Inspector David Owen." He added his first name in the hope it would help her relax. "Thank you very much for coming in. The public are such a vital link to solving many local crimes. Believe me, you will not be wasting anyone's time here today. Please come this way, it's more comfortable and a little less clinical." The warmth of his smile helped her relax as he opened the door allowing her to enter first.

The small lounge-type area was certainly less formal. A female support officer was already in the room. She stood as they both entered and Owen introduced her before explaining her role during their chat. Owen saw the stiffness in Carrie's shoulders ease.

"I saw your post on the police website, you know, the one about the youth seen in the garden on Langcliffe Avenue. I believe I saw him at about that time. Stood next to him on the bridge." She continued to explain the circumstances.

"How old would you say he was?" Owen leaned forward clasping his hand on his knees.

"Not old, say twelve or thirteen. About my height. I cross the bridge daily, Mr Owen. I work in a gym on Hornbeam Park. If it's a good day I find that a pleasant walk. I need fresh air as I'm stuck indoors all shift."

"Indeed. Now this is a long shot but have you seen the youth before or any others in that area particularly near or on the line?"

Carrie Wilkinson paused. "I've seen them around the station and the car park by the gym. I assumed they attended the college but I can't say I've seen him. The primary school's just over the way too." She paused giving further thought to her recollections. "The more I come to think of it there are kids on bikes stopping and chatting near groups of school children." She looked at Owen as if a lightbulb had illuminated. "They could have been passing things between them. Working in a gym I'm very much aware that drugs are readily available."

Owen looked at the support worker who had taken notes of the conversation. He fished into his top pocket and retrieved a card, straightened it before handing it to Carrie. "If you see anything again, I'd appreciate a call. My mobile is on there. Remember, you will not be wasting police time. Do you have children, Mrs Wilkinson?"

"No, not as yet. I'm not sure I want to bring kids into this world at present." Taking the card, she slipped it into the sleeve of her mobile phone. "I will, Mr Owen. If I can help, I will."

***

The process had been carefully and scientifically planned for quite some time. The procedure had been carried out on a couple of occasions but this would be the last time. The written lesson plan was attached yet again using a drawing pin securing the paper to the wall above the bench. The diagrams were crude but had all the hallmarks of a child writing up a chemistry experiment, listing the steps, apparatus, method and results. The prediction was omitted as the outcome was already known. The bowl containing the five hundred grams of specifically selected plant material was placed next to the small camping stove. A pan containing three hundred millilitres of distilled water was just coming to the boil and the plant material was added. The old kitchen timer was started and the reassuring mechanical tick seemed to accompany the bubbling water. Surprisingly, there was no really strong aroma but then the window was open and the door propped ajar by the fire extinguisher. The guidance had been thorough as chemistry skills never leave a trained teacher and the planning took account of all the necessary safety procedures and protocols.

The timer sounded. As the gas was turned off, the pan was removed to be placed on the heat-resistant mat that had come from a school near Knaresborough if memory served correctly. Asbestos, used for years in the school labs, had suddenly fallen foul of the new Health and Safety regulations. The solution needed to cool. A coffee was needed.

Looking west, the late evening was beginning to streak orange and grey as the low sun blushed the underbelly of the clouds. The trees and the visible rooftops stood in stark contrast, silhouetted and cold. The coffee, laced with some rum, proved to be the tonic required. It was a habit worth adopting. Entering the shed a hand reached for the light switch and the fluorescent tube spluttered and blinked into life highlighting the confused mess even more. The liquid, now cooled, was poured through a coffee filter and into a clean coffee jar. Care was taken to leave as much of the plant material in the pan as possible. Holding the pan handle so the pan was on the bench and with a potato masher in the other hand, the mulched material was crushed to extract the last of the fluid before the freshly squeezed liquid was poured back over a new filter paper.

Holding up the jar to the light, the brown tinged liquid in the jar was only just transparent. It was now time for the real chemistry to begin.

The bottle, marked *Chloroform,* was lifted from the shelf and the stopper removed and brought up to the nose. The smell was still sweet even after the years it had sat on the shelf. Stored correctly, it would be good for five plus years. A measure of the contents was added to the jar and was stirred vigorously before being allowed to stand. It was a time to reflect and finish the coffee. The previous crystallisation of the extract from Oleander and Monkshood had worked well.

"One must take small steps, slowly, slowly to catch your monkey." The words were thoughtful, yet said out loud to an empty room. "It's had to be more a toe in the water than a dive, after all, it's never good to bellyflop, not at my age and certainly not in public!" The words brought with them a chuckle. "That should be a sinister laugh, not a chuckle. After all, killers are meant to be evil." Reflecting on the creation of the concentrated solution of Monkshood brought a stop to the one-way conversation. The end result had been the real achievement. The viscosity was perfect and better than hoped for but then help had been close at hand. Like all processes there could not be, and neither should there be, any rushing. Watching the chloroform and water separate never ceased to amaze, the layers were perfect, like oil on water. The chloroform had trapped the particles once held within the aqueous solution. It was now back to improvisation. Using a turkey baster, the water was carefully drawn off leaving only the chloroform solution in the jar. This was then placed in a bain-marie, a double boiler, allowing the chloroform to be gently heated within the jar so that it could evaporate and allow the suspended contents to crystalise. This was the dangerous part as the venting fumes from the process could be extremely hazardous. The door and the window were opened more widely.

Outside the air was significantly cooler. The odd star now pierced the darkness. Looking up suddenly brought with it a dizziness. A steadying hand was placed against the shed wall. Light from the town lit the area just enough to maintain the outline of the surrounding trees and roofs. On returning, the jar was removed to reveal a successful collection of crystals. This brought a strong feeling of satisfaction. The chloroform bottle was returned to the shelf, ensuring the glass stopper was secure. If this worked there would be no need to produce more. Here was enough for what was planned. Stretching, a hand leaned over and removed the paper pinned to the wall. It was screwed up and tossed into the dark corner of the shed. Like the Rosetta Stone, one day it might be found and all would be revealed.

Chapter Eight

Wednesday morning had dawned gutlessly. The low orange sun sulled with an unnatural petulance that seemed to keep it just above the horizon for longer than necessary, only to peer through the silhouetted leaves that shielded the lower side of the garden to the left of the kitchen window. A faint blood-orange glow spread along the perimeter of the clouds turning their grey white edge to a warm, deckled surround. It was good news for Stan as at least the sun was visible, unlike on the previous mornings.

Stan Cooper was a creature of habit and if it were Wednesday and the weather was favourable, it was always a day to be on the river, to fly fish for trout or grayling. It was the season of his favourite fish, the trout, but the open season was rapidly drawing to a close and he tried not to miss an opportunity.

September had always been a special month in Stan's calendar, ever since his college days. Those fun-filled days were now over fifty years ago, but he had always enjoyed the marked, seasonal change the month brought, especially the dawn mists. A poem came immediately to mind:

"And then the sun took a step back, the leaves lulled themselves to sleep and autumn was awakened." His whispered words, seemingly as breathless as the day, erupted from slightly parted lips whilst he maintained his gaze on the dawning sky. There was no one there to hear them. He had no idea from which recess of his memory he had trawled the poem but it seemed as clear and sharp in his mind as the day he had learned it. *Fifty plus years. You're getting bloody old, Cooper*, he thought, making him pause and look away from the garden. *A lot of water has passed under this bridge of life. And a lot of missed bloody fish!* He began to hum a tune and then added the occasional word or two. "Regrets, I've had a few ..." The humming grew louder. *It's hard to comprehend the speed at which one's life passes.* "My ... bloody ... way." He spread his arms as if performing the closing words and then the humming continued before he paused in further thought. Closing his eyes, he tried to bring the French words of the song to mind, only succeeding in pronouncing *Comme d'habitude*. That thought was quickly blurred to be replaced by a vision of a crying young woman. A gruff, an almost lewd chuckle erupted from between his lips. His eyes remained tightly shut as if on opening them he would lose the image he now saw. *Goodness me, I'd forgotten all about you, Felicity, yes, that's right, Felicity.* He let each syllable roll off his tongue. *You were such a pretty, probationary teacher of French who made a complete hash of things. You were failing miserably until your Uncle Stan helped you get out of the corner and remove your teacher's dunce's cap. You were so co-operative and grateful for those few weeks of my influence and help. God you were a poor classroom practitioner, but in the bedroom ... I remember a lack of enthusiasm but it didn't really matter, you understood that one good turn deserved another. After all, that was our deal, pretty Felicity, and you did finally pass.*

As if his conscience was pricked, he allowed the vision to fade by deliberately opening his eyes and looking at his hands. There was a slight tremor. *If she'd have grassed on you, your career would have been up in smoke.* That thought brought a faint feeling of guilt and it flushed through his body. *You were such a lecherous old bastard, Cooper. At one point in your life, you believed you were invincible. Life was rich and fun, you had it by the tail, full of risk, reward and excitement. You had, you thought, all the time in the world. You believed life and your career had endless horizons, and then, when the birthdays rolled round, you suddenly realised that there was a point when there was more life sitting behind you than in front ... And then the tongues started wagging.*

From being quite perky, the mental mist seemed to wrap his thoughts, strangle his enthusiasm and flood his mind with a moment of utter foreboding. The thought clearly contradicted the words of the song as he was transported back to the latter part of his career.

It was the anonymous accusations, the whispers and looks, or rather the lack of them. People, particularly women, deliberately failed to look him in the eye. The feeling of helplessness; he suddenly seemed an outcast. It blighted that time in his life and had a detrimental effect on his general health. His early leaving was not classed as a dismissal, as things of this nature could easily be and were often concealed, swept casually under life's carpet away from public scrutiny. It was to him, however, and to the many who knew him, seen as professional failure. Time and misdemeanours caught up as it did for others who had enjoyed their chauvinistic, management authority. It had been a different time. Had it been today, he knew matters would have been handled very differently. On the whole, he had been lucky and on reflection he had much for which to be thankful.

It was true that he had received the leaving gifts and the presentations for his years of service but few colleagues appeared at the gathering and if they did, their visit was brief, either for fear of implication or because of their dislike of him. The short article and photograph published within the local paper read more like an obituary than a celebration of loyal service. The announcement clearly stated early retirement due to ill health. It was, after all, still necessary to keep up appearances; those above had a duty to look after those who knew enough to bring others down. There was also the hope that he would go quietly and not lose face totally. Some cynics might have suggested it was too kind a gesture, however, he did secure an enhanced pension, and that to him, was compensation enough. It hurt knowing that some heard rumours, but knowing that many knew the truth hurt more and wounded him deeply. After all, he was just one of the boys; they had all walked in the same shoes, shoes they had shared for a number of years and encouraged each other in which to waltz.

Dragging himself from his thoughts he checked the weather again. The forecast was for a mostly dry day with growing cloud in the mid-afternoon and the occasional shower. He had checked the online site for the Birstwith river level recorder and it had shown a recording of 0.4 metres at 05.30 – the water level in the River Nidd. It was surprisingly low considering the heavy rainfall over the previous week but it was an accurate gauge and at that level, just below maximum, he believed it was borderline but safe enough to fish.

As usual, Radio 5 Live broke the kitchen's morning's silence, it was always on in the background but Stan Cooper was now neither listening nor interested. Switching on the radio as soon as he entered the kitchen had always been a habit like many other facets of his morning ritual. The noise from the kettle began to drown the traffic report as he prepared his flask and sandwiches. The tea would be brewed in the teapot before being transferred to a container. This would then be popped in the microwave whilst the flask was heated through with more boiling water; another ritual, an annoying habit to some but an essential and scientific process to Stan. Tea, in his opinion, had to be hot wherever it was drunk and of the correct strength and to do that, one needed to know the science.

He placed four small cheese and pickle sandwiches into a Tupperware box followed by two neatly folded pieces of kitchen roll, then packed an apple and a Tunnock's Caramel Wafer into a freezer bag. All was ready. Placing them into the wicker creel was his final task. He stared momentarily at the basketwork. Although somewhat pretentious and showing signs of wear, it had been a retirement gift from the Director of Education. Now there was a real friend. Two rods were already in the car along with the other vital pieces of fishing tackle. Leaving the house, he checked his watch. It was just after 9 am.

***

Cyril Bennett had not enjoyed his walk to work. Recently it had felt just that step too far. *You're getting old, Bennett. In the early days this was a cinch, you needed neither a bus nor car, just simple exercise.* The day was set to be pleasant.

He approached April as she waited by the water station. The bubbles glugged to the top of the container creating a similar sound as she filled her mug. Turning she saw him standing there. She had neither heard nor seen his approach.

"You're like the missing mist this morning, sir. Like smoke! A glass of Adam's ale?" She pointed to the handwritten note above the inverted blue water container before adding a comment. "Warm ale. The chiller stopped working last week and has still not been fixed!"

Cyril said nothing but shrugged his shoulders. He had no interest in water. "I'll pass, thank you, and also pass your comments on to the management."

"You looking for me, sir?"

"How's your gut feeling about the deceased, Dr Rigby. Still strong?"

After taking a sip of water she shook her head. "Nope. Took a look at the bench up by the church. I was hoping it would feed the feeling but it had the opposite effect. You know how it is. Win some, lose some."

He briefly explained his conversation with Julie and he immediately saw April stiffen as a smile of silent, congratulatory satisfaction crossed her lips.

"It would have been a first, sir, you know, if that feeling had been hollow, if that makes any kind of sense?"

Cyril nodded knowing just what she had experienced. It was a kind of sixth sense.

"I want you to look into their past, both your man and also Seex. We know they have a connection professionally.

Also keep Shakti up to speed. I've organised a white board to be positioned outside my room. Keep it updated during your initial investigation. If we receive definitive Forensic evidence to suggest anything other than natural causes, we'll augment the resources. Just tread carefully at this stage but make sure it's upgraded to Category Two and ensure all that that implies is carried out."

They walked together to April's desk.

"Please add this to the top of the board." She removed the note from the wall next to her desk. "This was written on the back of the bench. I have a photograph and some memorial plaques that were also there. I think, however, this was a recent addition. Could be nothing but I'm keeping an open mind."

"You're learning, DI Richmond. Good to see your time with this department has not been a total waste!"

Cyril considered the initials and the '88' as he fixed the note to the board but at that moment it meant nothing to him.

***

The whole of the edge of the jigsaw was in place and most of the sky. From the picture it could be seen there was still much to do. It was a personalised puzzle bought some years ago. It had been completed once before when it was new. This time, however, it was proving a little more difficult.

***

The place Cooper planned to fish was a swim he knew well. The Nidd at Holme Bottom was usually quiet. He used to like fishing near Hampswaite, but the river bank was more popular with dog walkers. On occasion, he had found that dogs had a thing about people in waders and could get quite uppity. The quieter spots were his chosen places to spend the day.

The B6165 was relatively quiet as he approached the reflective roadside marker post just after the turning that would take him to the river. A minute or two after turning, he approached the disused railway line, now a cycleway and footpath. The gates that once closed the lane from the pathway were now in disrepair and left open. He continued to drive with caution. Passing the stone farm buildings to his right signalled he was nearly at the river. There were no other cars and it appeared he had the stretch of water to himself, at least for the moment. It could get busy on fine days so close to the trout season's end.

Collecting his things, he locked the car. His angling club pass was left clearly displayed on the dashboard. Once kitted up, it would take him five minutes to walk to his favoured peg. There he could leave his belongings secure on the bank and wade the river in the hope of catching a trout or two before lunch.

The sun penetrated the trees and dappled the clear, brown-tinted river. The rapids to his right gave the water a voice and he leaned on his wading staff, relaxing for a moment to soak up the atmosphere. Watching the light create patterns on the pebbles below the flowing surface proved mesmerising. Often these moments were as precious as the fishing itself. But it was the darker, deeper pools he wanted to fish and he moved his focus to one. A trout broke the dark, watery skin just away from the far bank leaving only a bubble and rings. *Is there a better place to be than here on a warm September Wednesday?* He doubted there was. He could hardly wait to get started.

When the familiar white Volvo crossed the cycleway a hundred metres ahead, the cyclist came to a halt with both feet placed firmly on the tarmac. Known to be a creature of habit, Stan's Wednesday routine was happening as predictably as clockwork. He would pass the farm buildings soon and then park in his usual spot.

Although the cycleway was bordered by trees, the view towards the distant man leaving his car was clear across the sloping field. It was easy to see Stan walk the gap between the edge of the field and the river bank to his favoured fishing spot.

Fifteen minutes later the bicycle was leaned against the wooden shed to the side of the parked car. The only sound came from the birds and the tumbling water in the shallows. Following the path taken by Cooper he soon clearly became visible. By watching through the thick bushes at the field's edge, not getting too close Cooper was observed sipping from a cup, the top of his flask. Patience, patience.

Throwing the dregs into the grass, Cooper replaced the cup back on his flask, checked his fishing tackle and entered the water. Within minutes he was facing downstream and mid-river, the rod moving gracefully in sweeping arcs; the water to his upper thighs brought slight waves. On his back was strapped his landing net and his wading staff floated attached to his jacket. The concentration was obvious as he cast, the fly line snaking bright green across the water's surface. His other rod and creel were left by the fence. All as normal.

There was little fear of being seen in the brief walk to the belongings left on the bank, as Cooper was now in a position downstream and towards the far bank, behind bushes overhanging the water's edge. No one else was about.

Nimble fingers undid the buckle holding the creel's lid, then removed and opened the flask. A wisp of steam escaped like a last breath before quickly vanishing, but in its wake it left the smell of strong tea. What was added would neither affect that nor change its taste, and if it were noticed as an after taste it would be too late.

Five minutes later Cooper could be seen from specific vantage points along the cycle path, still seeming too intent on watching and feeding out the line to see or hear anything else. Apparently he was in his heaven but that would soon change.

Chapter Nine

The Coach and Horses was quiet, no music, no games, no machines, just good beer and conversation if you needed it. On this occasion, Cyril needed some time alone before Owen arrived and he had built this into his schedule. He found a corner table, ran his finger around the rim of the glass and studied the amber transparency of the beer. It had been two days since the accident; the crash had occurred a moment's walk from where he was sitting. It played on his mind and continued to torment his thoughts. To think the mother had been dead two days … two whole days. His musings grew darker.

"I'll get my own shall I, sir?" Owen, oblivious and insensitive to his boss's private thoughts, destroyed the moment of reflection. His voice was bright and of the present and the enthusiasm in his words immediately lifted Cyril from his temporary, emotional morbidity.

"Thanks, Owen. I've opened a tab. Julie, and I believe Hannah, are popping in too and we're going to eat. There's curry on tonight."

Within a matter of minutes, Owen was back carrying two pints. The table wobbled as he tried to slide his knees under. Cyril instinctively grabbed his own pint to stop its demise.

"Sorry! Clumsy! Cheers!" The glass was tilted back and half the contents immediately disappeared. "Bloody hell, I was ready for that." He turned and looked at Cyril whilst removing the froth moustache with the back of his hand. "How heavy is the head that wears the crown? You don't seem your usual self, sir?" He finished the first pint putting the empty glass on the window sill. "Safe there."

"Hollow legs I see, Owen."

"Thirsty, sir, spitting feathers, I was. Are you okay?"

Cyril's look spoke volumes. "I didn't come into this job to shove paper about and justify every bloody penny spent. Besides, the speech is *Uneasy lies the head* ... Never mind, when did you last read Henry IV Part Two?"

"Who?" Owen started on his second pint.

"Julie called me today and asked me to pop over. Our two deaths may well turn out to be not as simple as we've been led to believe. Too many similarities. That's also backed up by Caner's medical expertise."

"I told you April had a nag. I don't think I've known her have a false call. Speaking of call, I need a pee."

Cyril raised an eyebrow as his hands instinctively held tightly onto the edge of the table. He watched as Owen slid his knees away before walking towards the bar. Picking up his pint, Cyril felt his phone vibrate, it was quickly followed by its piercing ring. It was Brian Smirthwaite.

"Bennett." Cyril's direct response would never change.

"Brian, sir. Sorry to call but I knew you'd want to know that we have another body." Smirthwaite paused allowing the information to sink in. "Male, sir, late sixties."

"Who? Where?"

"A Mr Stanley Cooper. Found floating in the river just upstream from Bilton Viaduct, close to the sewage works outlet. I'm unsure as to the exact location but he's in the water. April's gone out there and I believe a Forensic team will soon be there."

"Next of kin?"

Owen came back but remained standing. Cyril held up a finger.

"His wife's been notified. No kids. They've been separated for some time. Liaison Officer is there now. It's believed that he's a creature of habit and if that's the case he would have left to go fishing about mid-morning. Member of the angling club. His car's been located on the angling club parking area so the body's travelled some distance if we presume that he started fishing close to that spot."

"Why has April gone?" Cyril asked, knowing the answer the moment he had asked the question. "A Detective Sergeant would have done."

"According to her, he was a colleague of both Rigby and Seex. She'd already started researching the careers of the first two victims and Cooper's name was on a couple of the lists. She mumbled something about lightning not striking the same place thrice!"

"Keep me up to speed ... and Brian, who found the body?"

"Someone photographing the river from the viaduct. They used a telephoto lens after spotting something midstream."

"Thanks."

Looking through his contacts, Cyril called April. It rang for some time before she answered.

"April. You there?"

"I'm on the viaduct now but the light is fading fast. I've

checked the photographs taken by the chap who first spotted the body on screen. Just below me there's a fishing rod in the water trapped against one of the middle piers, probably belongs to the poor soul. Forensics have accessed the river via the sewage works giving them the best possible approach to the scene. I've also called the fire lads to assist with the removal of the body once the doctor and the Forensic team are happy that all the evidence has been collected. This area of the bridle way up to the lane leading to where his car is parked has been closed off and will remain so until tomorrow. I'll be heading down to the river bank after this call."

"Keep me informed. And April, whatever the time."

Cyril dropped his mobile onto the table as Owen squeezed into his seat opposite.

"Another body, Owen, and another member of the educational establishment. Why do my instincts now scream blue murder? Someone, my dear friend, is beginning to get even. I've been in this job far too long not to believe that one of their fellow academics is righting wrongs." He took a swig of his pint. "You mark my words."

"Do we have a name, sir?"

"Cooper, a Stanley Cooper."

Fortunately, on hearing the name, Owen had just brought the glass to his lips and had not started drinking. "Cooper? That name rings a bell. Rigby's son mentioned a Stan Cooper being an old friend of his father. Said something about encouraging his career choice. It'll be in the report ..."

"Have you two boys been sent into this corner for misdeeds?" Julie grinned as Owen clambered to his feet causing another small tsunami. "Hannah's on her way."

Owen never finished his answer but Cyril had already made a mental note and was putting two and two together.

***

For the first time in as long as he could remember, Cyril did not walk to work. He had called for a car to collect him and drive him to Holme Bottom. He liked to see the places where crimes might have taken place, to get a feel, to sniff around, *just to be on the safe side*, he always protested. Fortunately, the day had dawned fine. The police tape still fluttered, a visual, if somewhat feeble, barrier across the track left of the bridlepath heading to the river. A police vehicle was positioned a little further down. Collecting some protective clothing, Cyril lifted the tape. The Crime Scene Team had further protected the area around the white Volvo and the operative was enjoying a moment leaning against the van. Cyril waved. He would not need the overshoes if he stayed out of the enclosed area.

Although Cyril did not recognise the suited man, he seemed to know Cyril immediately.

"DCI Bennett if my memory serves me correctly."

Bennett nodded. "My reputation precedes me!"

"We met at the Grey House B&B if you recall, sir. The escape room deaths."

Cyril stared at the man as he remembered various cases until there was a sudden moment of accurate recollection. "Three keys, yes, The Grey House. Strange case, that. What do we have here?"

"Maybe another one but this death could be just accidental. He left his car here before walking down by the side of the far field." He pointed in the general direction.

"The equipment he wasn't carrying with him whilst fishing, and he was carrying a lot as fly fishers do, some was found tucked in the bushes just beyond that collection of coarse scrub. It would appear he died post lunch as his sandwich box was empty and only a biscuit wrapper remained in the box. The flask was empty too. An apple core was retrieved from the grass a short distance from that spot. We've marked it and it's numbered. I'll hazard a guess it was his."

An apple for the teacher, came immediately to Cyril's mind. "It's being tested – the apple core?"

A look of surprise flashed over the man's face as if his integrity were being challenged. "That, and the containers have been taken for analysis. That's what we do. That's our job."

Cyril realised he might have offended the man's professionalism. "Right, yes, sorry. No offence meant. Do you think it could be an accident?"

"I believe fishing whilst wading can be quite hazardous. The river base here comprises limestone pebbles. There are quite a few ledges and drop offs too; steep shelves on the river's bed that could catch out the clumsy or unstable. It doesn't matter how many times you fish, the river bed is constantly changing and reshaping so you need to be cautious at all times, particularly when fishing alone."

They both walked down to the river edge.

"So, you feel it could well just be accidental, a slip?"

The CSI raised his hands, his mood quickly improved. "As you know, our job is to collect the evidence piece by piece and then see if those elements fit. At this stage, only a gambler would speculate. He could have slipped, banged his head and drowned. As you said, accidents can happen.

It takes only a moment's lapse in concentration. We see it all the time."

Cyril's thoughts darted briefly to the young mother spread on the road, before focusing his mind on the task in hand.

"Any other cars or people here yesterday?"

"Checking the tyre marks, I can say cars came to the farm buildings back there up the track and we've taken samples of a cycle tyre discovered in the soft ground behind the car. Any footprints have also been sampled and we should have those results to you later."

***

The shrill scream of the boiling kettle could be heard in the garden. Secateurs clipped another small section of root from the side of one of the shrubs. It, along with the cutters, were tossed into the trug followed by the gloves. "If Pavlov calls." The gas was turned off and the whistling slowly died. The trug was placed on the table by the trays as another piece of the jigsaw was spotted – it fitted straight in.

***

Cyril's car turned down Beckwith Head Road. The Harrogate Police Station was to the left. The driver stopped close to the steps to the main entrance. On climbing out, Cyril tapped the roof as if in thanks.

He immediately went to his office. The white board on the easel was still there but on it was written:

All the details transferred to Incident Room 2.

April was writing notes on one of the wall boards when he entered. She turned, smiled and then carried on. Neither spoke until she had finished.

"Sorry. Morning, sir." She tapped the photographs on

the board with the capped marker pen. "Fishing. Who'd have thought it could kill you?"

Cyril moved to look at the images. They had been taken when the body was in the water.

"They carry a good deal of tackle. The vest, waders, landing net. That's a wading staff to help keep your balance, according to one of the ancillary staff who also is a keen fly fisher."

"Didn't help keep his balance did it!" Cyril turned his head at an angle to bring perspective to the photograph as the body was horizontal. "Who? Which ancillary?" he asked, his focus still on the body in the water.

"Georgie Eadington, civilian admin. She knows the stretch of water and has fished it many times. She's seen the images and what he's carrying is, I'm assured, normal practice. She assured me you have to be prepared for every eventuality. Strange game. They usually put the fish back too. It's all in the chase apparently."

"A bit like this job. I don't take that much clobber when I go for a week's holiday, April, let alone if I'm going to wade up to my waist in cold, fast flowing water. May as well carry a bag of cement too!"

April chuckled. "Exact time of death has been difficult to ascertain owing to most of the body being immersed. As you know, the cold plays strange tricks on the dead. It was lucky it was spotted so quickly. Remaining undiscovered for a couple of days would have made the pathologist's life even harder. As you see, the clobber he's wearing was greeny-brown in colour and would camouflage the body against his surroundings. You could imagine if the body had been washed under an overhanging, semi-submerged branch, it might not have been spotted for days."

"Injuries?"

"Not that we know of." April moved to the nearest computer. "We have people at his home now ensuring it's secure. The neighbour saw him leave just after nine. She told us he usually waits for the school run to subside. Knowing his old job, I can empathise with that, sir."

"Long shot. Was there a note?" Cyril asked knowing the answer and believing this would not be suicide.

"Only one left on the kitchen table, a reminder to cancel the milk on Friday. At this stage I suggest we keep it a Category Two Sudden Death. It can be moved to Cat One if the evidence is found. Because of that, we're holding back on a full Forensics overview in case it's just accidental or natural causes. When we hear from the pathologist and the coroner, we can respond and if necessary, get the wheels moving."

Cyril nodded. Their budget was constrained enough. "Show me the links to the other two deaths. I take it these are all now computerised? As a thought, did Cooper carry a phone?"

April did not answer immediately but went towards another board. "None found to date. All three employed around the same time. They were classed under the procedures for Sudden Death Category Three but I'd like to see them revised to Category Two as I know you've done with Rigby. Depending on the findings with Cooper, move them all to Category One which will allow for greater resourcing."

Cyril exhaled. "I do hope you have strong evidence to justify that. You'll need it. You're SIO?"

April nodded. "For the time being. I'll get the necessary paperwork in place and the reports to the coroner today."

"Anything on Cooper's car?"

"As yet it's pending with Forensics on our findings. I have links to the LEA records to search for further details. I've also asked for a list but more likely it will probably be lists of those working with them, including those teaching within the authority in their last five years as all three left within a short time scale. Once we have that information, we'll filter for those still alive, those local and work outwards. Tech people are checking their social media links and contacts. They were not only colleagues but friends away from work. They're now collecting details from their internet and their phone records."

"Well done. And Shakti?"

"She's at his address and talking with neighbours. We might find a little more about his personal life."

"Keep busy." Cyril, put up a thumb and left.

Chapter Ten

Owen sat opposite Sonia Dawson. He could see that she was nervous. To his left was a female officer. The introductions had been brief.

"Thanks for coming in. It's your son you want to talk about?"

She nodded, looking down at the clasped hands on her lap. Owen could see her left knee bouncing with nerves.

"I didn't know whether to come in. He's my son and I'm talking to the police about him as if he's a criminal. I'm frightened for him and I'm scared for my other kids but I'm more scared for me." She paused. "Does that make me selfish?" Not waiting for the answer, she continued, the words flowing quickly yet with uncertainty. "He's changed." She looked up, briefly glancing first at Owen and then turning her gaze to the officer. It lingered there for some time. Nothing was said. Time seemed to hang. After a couple of false starts she eventually blurted out a full sentence.

"I think he's dealing drugs." Taking a tissue from her sleeve she wiped her nose before sniffing. Her eyes were now planted on Owen.

"Firstly, Mrs Dawson, if this is what you suspect then you've done the right thing. I know it's not easy but you're helping all those you mentioned. Does your husband suspect this also?"

"I've been a single parent since my husband died in a motorcycle accident just over three years ago. It was the day everything changed for us. Life could never be the same again and it affected us all badly. At first, Martin couldn't accept his father would not be coming home. When it hit him, he ripped all the posters of bikes and riders from his bedroom wall. He was a ball of anger. He did receive some help. So, I suddenly had to bring up my three kids alone and after a rocky twelve months things started to seem okay, we were doing just fine until ..." She broke down again but soon managed to regain her composure. "He's changed, our Martin. Six months ago, he wouldn't say boo to a goose. Now he's moody and disobedient, seems to have more money than he should. He's always late in. I tried to give him a clip round the ear when he was insolent but he grabbed my wrist. He hurt me too. Do you know, that was something his father never did? It frightened me I can tell you."

"Do you know if he takes drugs?" Owen asked. He ensured his voice remained strong to give her the necessary assurance she needed in this weakened state in which she found herself. It was something he had learned from Cyril over the years.

She shook her head. "I've not found any on him but he's a bright lad. Always near the top at school until this all kicked off. They've contacted me a couple of times about his disrespectful attitude in school and the classroom. He was excluded for four days a few weeks back. He just didn't seem bothered. In fact, it was the school who suggested I come to you. They said you'd have specialist liaison people who'd work with him."

"We do and we will. You need some support too. Is Martin in school today?"

"He should be and they've not contacted me to tell me any different."

As if it were planned, her mobile rang. The ring tone was a piece of modern music but Owen failed to recognise it.

"Please answer it," Owen requested. He watched her expression. He caught the occasional muffled word from the phone but Sonia's facial expression said it all.

"I don't know if he's gone home. I'm not at home. I'm at the police station. You suggested I speak with the police. When did you last see him?"

Owen glanced at the female officer and then back towards Sonia Dawson as she slipped the phone onto her lap.

"He's gone missing from school, they think just before lunchtime. He wasn't in the first lesson after the break." Cupping her face in her hands she began to weep. Owen heard the long, drawn-out sob and then her shoulders shook. "I need your help before he gets into serious trouble if he's not already – or worse – I've seen on the television what can happen with knives and the rival gangs. Please! Please!"

It was a plea that Owen could not refuse. He felt a lump appear in his throat as she spoke so earnestly. Within minutes they had a description and photographs from her phone. Initially, the boy's absence would not be broadcast to the public but the information was distributed to those in the force. Within the hour every officer on duty would be carrying his digital image and a description of Martin

Dawson.

***

April had forwarded the pathologist's report to Cyril. It had been written more quickly than expected. Owing to the possible link with the two previous deaths, April had requested the coroner agree to an urgent post-mortem to be carried out on Stanley Cooper after the upgrade in Sudden Death Status to Category One – death involving suspected offences. On this occasion, the request had been accepted and the coroner supported it. It clearly stated that this was a preliminary assessment to confirm the belief that there were similarities with the previous two deaths. It was the words *toxic substances* that made Cyril sit up. He remembered Julie's words: *If I were to hazard a guess right now, it would be some kind of toxic substance.* Scratching his head momentarily before picking up his pen, he scribbled on his jotter pad what else he remembered from the conversation. *Toxic can mean overindulgence of a substance to the point where it's detrimental to the person's health.*

"Whatever it was, it was certainly detrimental to Cooper's health," he grumbled loudly before continuing to digest the report, only to be disturbed by a knock on his door. It was April.

"Have you seen this report?" She tapped the few sheets of A4 she held in her hand.

Cyril pointed to his computer screen. "It's here. Just reading it now. Looks like we have number three. If it's murder, and like your initial tingling gut, I strongly believe it is, whoever's doing the killing is both efficient and effective. Something tells me the chances are it's likely to be another teacher. I'll wager a tenner. It's orderly and it appears to be clinical. The simple questions are who, with what and why?"

"The holy trinity of *Cluedo* and more importantly, still used in modern police investigation, sir."

April's comment brought a smile.

"Hopefully, sir, once toxicology has concluded their investigations, we'll have one of the answers."

"The easy one. I hope!"

"Something came in from Forensics that gave me the shivers." She placed two photographs before him. "Cooper's vehicle is being assessed and they sent these. If you look carefully it appears someone has smudged the dirt on the rear paintwork. Our Mr Cooper was not a Sunday car wash chap. They are letters and numbers spread over the back. They're faint but they are made up of UR/WYS 91. We found similar markings on the bench where Rigby died."

Cyril chipped in. "But '88' and not '91'."

"Forensics are certain this was in place before the day he was found as there's additional road dirt over the markings. They believe one or two days. If this is the case, the death was planned and executed by someone who knew his routine."

"Rigby's was written on the bench. A thought, April. Was Rigby a regular walker and if so, did he follow the same route? Secondly, have we looked at other benches, walls, potential seats on that route. If his death were planned how on earth could they predict he'd sit where he did unless the tag was added afterwards? After all, the initial inspection was neither thorough nor necessary. Check with the officer who filled out the G28 form. The work load grows in direct proportion to the paperwork." Cyril tapped the pile sitting in his *In* tray. "We need answers to certain questions to make the fragments fit."

"Promotion can be a burden, taking many away from what they do best, sir. Uneasy lies …" She did not finish the quote. Cyril's expression was enough. She turned to leave.

"That's the second time I've heard that. I don't see a crown, April. When I was a nipper, we had a ritual at home that was performed after the evening meal. My father brought home a Mars Bar daily and it was dissected into three pieces. The fact that there were only the three of us was convenient because my father repeatedly told of the advertising slogan Mars once used for that particular confectionery. What do you think it said?" He looked at April who shook her head. "Like me, you're far too young to know of course: *A Mars a day helps you work, rest and play.* As soon as we had each nibbled our pieces, I was sent to do my homework. The piece I received was always the *work* section. Mother always received the *rest* and father … he'd bugger off and from what I discovered later … went off to *play.* And so, April, the moral of this little family vignette that I'm sharing for the first time?" He paused but not long enough to receive an answer. "Julie mentioned to me that if you have too much of anything it becomes toxic. I could never face a Mars Bar after I left home. They signified work and usually lots of it, but more importantly, it also reminded me of my father's choice of play. However, I did work extra hard, hard enough to forget that difficult part of my childhood. When Wendy, my stepmother, came on the scene the ritual ceased." Looking up at April he raised one eyebrow and returned his gaze to the screen.

For the first time in a long time, she felt uncomfortable in his presence, it was the uncertainty as to whether to speak or just leave. She chose the latter, understanding a little more of the psychological damage parents can heap on their children. It also made her consider the three deaths and she pondered whether these three had heaped any damage either physical and mental, on any of the children they taught over the years. If that were the case then they were dealing with many potential suspects. She made a note to see if any legal complaints had been lodged against them during their careers.

***

Shakti's report from her visit to Cooper's neighbours had brought one or two important points of interest to the investigation. Cooper had lived in the house for a considerable number of years. Some neighbours had been reluctant to gossip, but others seemed to enjoy the opportunity to shed light onto a world that they could not condone. Certainly, with one particular neighbour, Cooper had in the past sown the wind and Shakti was clearly interviewing a woman scorned.

The Coopers, she had been informed, had a second home, believed to have been left by his parents. It was situated in Knaresborough and Ingrid, Mrs Cooper, had moved there when they divorced. On the relevant whiteboard, Shakti had highlighted the fact that both Rigby and Cooper were divorcés; it was a potential common denominator. There was also talk of a number of women coming to the home after his wife had moved out. According to the one neighbour, some stayed for what seemed like months before vanishing whilst others were fly-by-nights. The neighbour furnishing Shakti with the information could only recall first names. Each name was given and Shakti had noted the degree of vitriol within the neighbour's voice as each name was offered. These names were added to the board: Pippa, Susan and a Zoe but she was aware that without surnames or further details they would bring nothing to the investigation. There were others, but the neighbour could neither remember their names nor could she describe them.

Surprisingly, the neighbour at number twelve, who had been happy to furnish Shakti with the facts, had suddenly broken down as their interview was coming to an end. The stony facade just crumbled and it was clear to Shakti that she still had a candle burning within for Cooper.

DC Nixon pushed open the Incident Room door with his foot. He carried a mug of coffee in one hand and a sausage roll in the other. His eyes smiled at his colleague as he finished what he was eating.

"Had a look at the notes on Cooper and like his name suggests, Shak, he's a bit of a racy character." He took another bite from the roll.

Shakti's expression told him she had not understood the connection.

"Cooper, you know, Cooper made racing cars way back. We still have the Mini Cooper. Comes from the race car designer, John Cooper. Built great cars, they were fast and championship winning." Holding the remnants of the sausage roll towards the whiteboard, he concluded his observation. "He seemed like his name, a fast worker. That was my point. With the women, Shak." The last piece of pastry was pushed into his mouth and he turned away.

"The neighbour at number twelve has clearly been

emotionally damaged by him so to use your analogy, she crashed and burned sometime in the past. I need to have a longer chat with her when she settles and we have more info. Knowing the right time is key."

Chapter Eleven

Owen tapped his finger on the youth's image. "Missing kids tend to get priority and the face of Martin Dawson should have been spread all over the police website and social media sites as you know, but for tactical reasons, we're not doing that for now." Owen did not expand on his reasoning but both officers were aware that owing to the sensitive nature of the situation and the possible link with the movement of drugs and county line gangs, the decision had been made to hold back posting his face everywhere. That could compromise the boy's position if he were in a gang and potentially endanger his wellbeing.

DC Shakti Misra and DC Henry Jones stood facing Owen's desk as he briefed them. They were to visit Martin's school and receive an updated report on his deteriorating behaviour. School absences might correlate with the reported sightings. They would also visit his home and look through his wardrobe, collecting items of clothing that might be linked to those seen being worn by the youth on the CCTV images. DNA could also be taken once back at the station.

Owen knew his officers would respond sensitively but he emphasised the urgency of the situation and that they needed to work with speed. Either Martin would walk back through his front door as if nothing had happened, or he might never be seen again. The number of missing persons, especially young girls, was a disturbing situation that constantly frustrated the police forces around the UK. As they left, he made his way to Cyril's office to update him.

"Remember this, Owen. It was said to me years ago by one of my flying instructors. Falling is like flying … it's only when you hit the ground do you know the difference. We'd been talking about drugs and he came out with that and it's stayed with me ever since. Kids selling drugs or acting as mules, get a great buzz. Suddenly, they think they are someone, a big shot with money, they believe they're soaring above their peers." He paused looking squarely at Owen, expecting a response.

"Only they're falling, sir. They're out of control?"

"Exactly. The frightening thing, my friend, is we must never forget the mess they leave for the family when they hit the ground. We need to find your Martin Dawson and all the other kids who think they're a modern-day Biggles and untouchable."

***

April organised for the wives of Rigby and Cooper to be interviewed at home. She was determined to see them on the same afternoon and organised Nixon to accompany her. There was no specific order as it would depend on their availability on a certain date.

***

Owen parked outside his apartment and sat back in the car, his head on the seat headrest, the lights turned off. He stared ahead whilst continuing to drum lightly on the steering wheel. He thought of Sonia Dawson and her face etched with a cruel anguish. It brought to mind a question. *Am I truly equipped to reassure the poor woman that her son will be found and if so, he'll be found safe and well?* He had acted according to what he knew to be police practice, considering the circumstances, by putting the protocols and procedures from his training into place. He knew, however, that there could be no promises made to her or anyone else and that included himself. That hurt. Fate would play a part and that was something he never understood nor did he want to. "What will be, will be," he said out loud. "If only they supplied crystal balls to each officer during their training!" He drummed the wheel and opened the car door.

He had phoned Hannah to say he would be late. It was her afternoon off and if he knew her like he thought he did, she would either have been shopping and keen and eager to show him her latest purchases, or curled up on the settee with a book or film. The thought of her brought some comfort and put a spring back into his step. He had told her he would be back at eight and he was close, only eleven minutes late. He crossed the courtyard towards the Victorian house that contained four apartments. They had secured the two bedroom flat twelve months after they had met, as they each had their own place to sell. The modern decor and the small garden, more like a yard, had attracted them and there was off-road parking for both vehicles.

Opening the door, the aroma struck him as soon as he entered. "Honey, I'm home," he mimicked in an American accent. "Something smells good."

There was no reply. The light was on in the hall. He tossed the keys in the large bowl, the crap bowl, as it was affectionately known. It contained all manner of items removed from pockets including keys, coins and business cards. Nothing was barred, everything seemed to find its way there and not everything deposited was removed – hence the title and the reason it was the first place of call when something went missing. "Hannah!" Owen called as he moved through to the kitchen following the source of the smell. The light from the oven spread a warm, yellow glow across the floor and the front of the surfaces and units. He called again and entered the lounge. The small dining table was set. It was then he saw her. She was on the settee. The television volume was set low and she was asleep. She had changed into pyjamas and a dressing gown. Moving quietly, he leaned over and kissed her forehead. Opening her eyes, a smile came to her lips.

"You look beautiful. I'm starving!" The mischievous grin spread as her hand instinctively moved to clip him at the side of the head.

"Me, first, not stomach, David Owen. You're a monster." Shaking her head, she sat up with his help and they kissed. "Wine's open and ready."

As he was pouring the wine, Hannah was busy in the kitchen. He remembered the first time he had seen her. Coincidentally, on that day she was at a crime scene close to the sewage works by the River Nidd, the same place Cooper had been found. She was working with Dr Julie Pritchett. It was a strange case. There had been the discovery of a missing child. He had watched her photographing the scene and he had been enchanted by her. Unusually for him, he had plucked up enough courage to ask her out for a drink but she had flatly refused. He had been rejected before but it was the way she had said no, it seemed cold and without any hesitation nor interest. He remembered the strong feeling of hurt but also the kind words of his colleague, Liz Graydon, who informed him that Hannah already had a boyfriend. She was a kind soul, Liz. The fleeting memory brought Martin Dawson back to the forefront of his mind.

Hannah came in with the chicken casserole. "Sit, big fella."

Owen did not need asking twice.

On completion of his meal, Owen picked up the napkin and wiped his mouth. Hannah had taught him something during their time together! "That was special. Thank you." He lifted his glass and pushed it across the table. "Cheers. I do love you, Hannah Peters. Do you remember the first time we met?"

"I showed you a photograph taken at a crime scene. It was of a jar of honey, if my memory serves me correctly."

"Yes, and I asked if you fancied a drink and you said, no thanks, as cold and as cruel as that. I was so hurt, cut to the very quick."

"Sorry!"

"Forgiven."

"Dreadful case that." She moved her hand across the table and covered his. "For a mother to find her child missing is just terrifying but then to be told ... How could they ever fully recover? I know I wouldn't. When I was a child, as you know, we lived in Easingwold. I remember on one occasion I couldn't get my own way and stormed out of the house after my mother and I had screamed at each other. Somehow, my mother and me never saw eye to eye from when I was twelve or thirteen until I matured. Anyway, I left the house slamming the door as hard as I could. I was determined never to return. I remember taking money I'd saved from my birthday and the previous Christmas."

"Where did you go?" Owen poured more wine into both glasses.

"York. I walked for quite some time before getting the bus. I knew York well and I had a best friend living there. I'd called her. I had to use a phone box as I didn't have a mobile then – life was so complicated. We stayed out as late as we could but then it rained and we were both wet, cold and to be honest, scared. Mum had called all my friends' parents. She was frantic but then received news that I was with Sophie. She knew I'd come home. Her dad brought me."

"And the consequences?"

"As a police officer, you don't want to hear. Kids got a clip in those days, believe me. I was grounded for weeks."

Owen started to clear the plates. "We have a missing kid at present. Twelve and rebellious. Sounds just like you only male so I don't know if that will make things better or worse for him. Same attitude towards his mother though."

Hannah followed Owen after clearing the rest of the table. "Hormones at that age. Dreadful things that can really screw you up. Disappearing, leaving home, is not the same these days. There are some unscrupulous people out there waiting to pick up the pieces and who can tempt kids as they go through the trauma that's adolescence. It can quickly get out of hand and be too late. I don't need to tell you that. The missing persons' statistics tell all. We've seen the results."

"His mother believes it to be drug related and she's scared daft. She has two other younger kids and to make matters worse, her husband was killed in a motorbike accident three years ago. Single mum, grafting hard and trying to do what's right without any training. There's no natural bloody justice."

"The poor woman. Sometimes I'd love to be a mum but then I feel I couldn't cope with bringing children into this crazy world."

Owen swung his arm round her and pulled her close. "I know just how you feel." The words of Carrie Wilkinson immediately came to mind and they mirrored Hannah's almost verbatim. He kissed her forehead and closed his eyes.

Chapter Twelve

The jigsaw on the second of the two trays was beginning to look more like the original picture on the box lid. The sky was now complete. Some foliage and blossom, a red flowery shrub, had grown over the few days in the bottom corner. Positioned on the first tray, those pieces showing red that might fit had been collected. The remaining pieces were now organised too; the figures, the clothes, colours and most importantly, the elements of the people's faces. Instead of the usual urgency to finish the puzzle it had seemed more important to bring the final pieces into some semblance of order. It would be done in good time, God willing!

***

"Poisoned, Cyril," Julie pronounced. "The toxicology results are clear for the first two. In both cases, Seex and Rigby were poisoned. Each died as a direct result of consuming a toxic substance that was similar but not the same for each. I've requested a Forensic assessment of Rigby's clothing. I'll explain the reasoning behind that on receipt of the information."

Cyril nodded, not questioning her professional thought process even though her diagnosis brought a degree of confusion. "So, in each case a different poison is what you're telling me?"

"More than likely according to the evidence, although both poisons may be from the same genus." She paused for a moment whilst waiting for Cyril to grasp the idea. "One of the medical similarities both victims displayed was a swollen or distended abdomen, ankles and legs, a clear indication their bodies were not working efficiently and therefore they suffered from oedema, retention of bodily fluids, Cyril. This is a result of both not having the strongest of hearts. Rigby's son reported that he used to cough a great deal but particularly over the last few months. His father believed it to be asthma until his doctor prescribed digoxin. This helped alleviate the continuous coughing but meant he had to urinate much more frequently."

"And the poisons? Obviously administered by someone who knew them both, met with them. Can we presume that?"

Julie just nodded. "Can we ever do so in cases of this nature?"

"I take it that it can't be left on door handles or park benches as that's too random." He paused considering where Rigby had been discovered and then remembered the Salisbury novichok attack. From what he could recollect the victims, a father and daughter, were found on a public bench. Two other people were also contaminated after finding a perfume bottle. "Remember Salisbury where one victim found a perfume bottle?" Cyril could not remember the finer details of the case. "Could this be similar?"

Julie knew the case well. The paperwork that flooded in after those poisonings was a stark and frightening warning to those who might meet similar cases in a medical or professional capacity.

"He found it in a litter bin and she tested it by spraying some of the contents on her wrist. Within fifteen minutes she was dead. The man was lucky to survive."

"We're not talking a type of nerve agent with these deaths? Please tell me that."

Julie shook her head. "Nothing so sinister. Rigby, Seex and probably Cooper were important to nobody apart from the one person who sought revenge. That would be my thinking. We know one of the poisons was a derivative of the plant, Oleander. It was noted during the autopsy that both Seex and Rigby had an excessive amount of undigested food in the gut, one of the symptoms. We, Caner and I, discussed the possible cause and he thought Abrin."

"Abrin?"

"I'll get there in a minute. Most of the Oleander plant is poisonous and it's known in Sanskrit as the 'Horse Killer'. Even the pollen can make the honey derived from Oleander poisonous. However, in Rigby's case it was not used in isolation. If you're a crime reader, and I know you're not, Cyril, it's a poison favoured by many authors. However, there's a twist here as there can be a latent period after administering it. It's now possible to discern which specific plant we're dealing with and that's key as many plant poisons contain digitalis glycoside. We think Rigby was given Abrin, one of nature's most toxic substances as this contains a tetanic glycoside."

Cyril held up his hands as if in surrender. "Julie, in plain, layman's terms."

"The poisons mentioned act over a period and that wouldn't do, it wouldn't kill him. You require a backup. You need something that will hit the bloodstream and within ten minutes you have your result. You have started the ball rolling with the initial poison. Rigby would not feel well, nauseous, probably a little giddy and dizzy. He would need to sit down, rest. The mouth ulcers would be aggravating. He might then take the next potion and that poison would cause the heart to fail."

"Next poison?"

"Remember the bottle found in his pocket?"

"The tincture?"

"Yes. A symptom of Oleander poisoning is the development of mouth ulcers and although I couldn't recall seeing them during the initial autopsy, I checked the file and images and they were present. They were believed to be a result of denture friction. Rigby had also recently had a tooth extracted and we've checked the reason for that with his dentist. He broke two teeth eating an almond. One tooth couldn't be saved and was extracted. I enquired if he had complained of any recent illness as normally the dentist will ask but he had said not. That bottle did contain what I mentioned – anaesthetic and antiseptic, but it also contained a highly concentrated distillation of Monkshood – *Aconitum napellus* is the Latin term to satisfy the pedant and botanist in you." Her sarcasm was not lost. "Symptoms begin rapidly and death can be within ten minutes depending on a number of conditions."

"For whatever reason he sat on the bench. If he then applied the tincture to the soft tissue of the raw and tender gum and rubbed it gently as prescribed on the bottle …"

"It rapidly enters the bloodstream," Julie responded.

"Enough to kill?"

"In the concentration toxicology discovered, yes, but he may have been applying contents of a similar bottle since the extraction and that then was probably poison free."

"Are you suggesting someone swapped the bottle or changed the contents?"

"I'm thinking out loud, Cyril, trying to make sense of it."

There was a lengthy pause as both Cyril and Julie put the evidence into perspective.

"Are most of these plants readily available?"

"They're all around us." Not wanting to sing to make her point she hummed the first part of the tune. "According to that song, *In an English Country Garden*, you'll find many toxic plants. There's even a Poison Garden in the north east not far from here. It's a kind of tourist attraction. I must take you there, Cyril. They might let you try before you buy!"

"Thanks. We'll be travelling south on our next holiday, my girl! And the other two?"

"Seex is a little more complex and we await further tests for Cooper."

***

The morning briefing was planned for an early start. There was much to discuss. Most attending would have checked the files and the recent whiteboard details and therefore they would be aware of much of the latest evidence and findings. The head table contained a number of strategically placed files. The projector screen illuminated the whiteboard behind the table, it glowed with the North Yorkshire Police crest which in turn cast a blue light onto the walls and papers.

A number of officers were already present either chatting in small groups or working their way through the files. April would be present but Owen was holding his own small team briefing, evaluating the evidence they had to date on the drug threat and the missing youth.

Cyril entered with Julie Pritchett. She had, after talking it through with Cyril, decided to keep her maiden name for professional engagements and work. She had a file carefully tucked beneath her arm. He smiled as he passed his colleagues and shared a word or two which brought some laughter. He did not sit but pulled a chair away from the table for Julie. She sat and a number of officers took their seats.

"Morning everyone. Thank you for the early start but I'm sure you're all aware of the latest findings. We're here to put those into perspective in order to focus our ongoing investigation into what is looking more like a double murder enquiry with the possibility of a third. Many here know Dr Julie Pritchett. She's kindly popped along to give you a clear picture of the complex nature of the way both Seex and Rigby were believed killed. I also wanted her to be able to answer your questions. We're not looking for a violent criminal but we are looking for a murderer and, not wanting to put ideas into your heads, this person could be of any age or sex. They'll have a good knowledge or an acquired knowledge of plant toxicology and the way those toxins can be extracted. We often forget that the hedgerows and woodlands that we so readily take for granted will hold some of nature's most potent poisons. The deadly killer, ricin, is the extract from a plant, the castor oil plant. I think my granny had one in her lounge for years. She used to polish the leaves and she lived well into her eighties. We must also remember that many of these plant extracts are used daily for the benefits of mankind. Many are medical ingredients and that can be a problem with autopsy diagnosis but I'll stop there not wanting to steal Dr Pritchett's thunder."

Julie Pritchett stood and spoke for fifteen minutes presenting the evidence. She included images taken during the autopsy before opening the room to questions. It was DC Dan Grimshaw who waved his hand.

"Dr Pritchett, I've done a little research since reading the notes." He pointed to the whiteboard. "Toxins derived from plant extraction is not an exact science and although they are graded owing to their toxicity, managing that is extremely complex. As you've said, many are used in everyday medicine. That used is finely managed. In these cases, we see here, according to the results," he held up the paperwork, "that both men were poisoned by different substances, two in Rigby's case. You mentioned the similar findings both you and your colleague witnessed during the examination. My point is, doctor, are we looking for a chemist or a lucky crank?"

A number of heads turned from Grimshaw to Dr Pritchett and some mumbling was heard.

"You need to consider that the person either knows or is acquainted with someone who does have the expertise to extract the required substances; it's not technically difficult because much can be achieved using materials in the raw state. You can also boil and concentrate as you would a stock when cooking. The difficulty comes when you need certain chemicals to aid the extraction. Many of those are watchlisted and their purchase will be monitored as happens with bomb-making materials. The tracking is now, as you're all well aware, very sophisticated. In their simplest form these toxic substances can be added to food or a drink by someone who has or creates the opportunity. DCI Bennett will not know this as he doesn't have a television." She turned to look at him and then back to her audience. "Remember the use of Lily of the Valley in *Breaking Bad*? Goodness, you'd have to be very lucky to get a result like they did and also, even though it's extremely toxic, it's rare that we ever see death from that specific plant. It's not what you have it's what you can do with it. This person is far more subtle. They have some knowledge of the victims' medical conditions. Both Seex and Rigby had heart issues, both were of a certain age and if you look at Cooper's medical history, he was in a similar category. My belief, at this stage at least, is the poisoner is an acquaintance, maybe once a friend but more likely someone who has been upset, scorned or abused in some way."

April interjected. "What about the possibility of a student who might have long held a grudge from his time teaching?"

"Bloody hell. That would open a huge list. Maybe it would be worth checking if there was ever a disciplinary action against any of the three or the LEA during this time."

Julie turned to Cyril knowing that time was pressing.

Cyril replied, "That's in hand. This is more than likely an act of revenge. Let's not forget that the perpetrator may not have intended death in the first instance. They might have just wanted to make them suffer."

"And it went wrong?" a voice from the group blurted out.

"That we may never know but let's all consider that we might not have a real expert, we might not have your chemist, we may well have the crank. What we do have, however, is someone who is determined and dangerous," Julie continued. "One final point. The Forensic tests on Rigby's clothing suggest he had vomited a number of times before sitting on the bench. There was spatter found on his shoes and lower trousers. There was also a tissue in his pocket. When he took to the bench, he was unwell." Julie turned to Cyril and tapped her watch and mouthing, *Sorry, time.*

Cyril quickly stood and thanked her as she left the room. A number of the officers added words of thanks as she left.

"April?" Cyril announced as he shuffled his file into some semblance of order.

April moved to the front. "Owen interviewed Rigby's son. Considering that information – page twelve of the file – we believe the person who killed Rigby, either worked for the same LEA as he at some stage in his career and ... this is one of the longest shots we could make, they went to the same college or university. After retiring early, Rigby joined a Facebook group comprising people who worked within this local authority. His son, at Rigby's request, helped establish the connection and worked with him until he was comfortable and confident enough to interact on the site unaided. He remembers some of the names of those within the group, in particular Mr Stanley Cooper. You're all now familiar with his death, found drowned whilst fishing. He also knew a couple of the others. He remembered Seex, but only because of the unusual name. But Cooper was a long-standing friend who visited their house. Both are linked to Rigby who now seems to take centre stage. We've requested access to his laptop and we'll identify those within the group over the period he was a friend."

"Thanks, April." Cyril stood and brought up a list onto the interactive whiteboard. "We've been trawling through the LEA list of employees and whilst trying to keep the numbers practical and relevant, we have these names. I've allocated them to you accordingly and they are in the files you received this morning. I want them checking. In particular I want to know if any one of those has suffered illness over the last twelve months that might prove to be poisoning. As we've heard, death might not have been the initial motive. Dr Pritchett has included in that file a list of questions you can pose to ascertain that specific answer. As far as Cooper is concerned and we've no reason to not believe he was a victim, we have some random names given by a neighbour. Let's say for politeness and political correctness, they were visitors to Cooper's home after his wife left. Although many are first names, let's see if we can find a possible match with those employed by the LEA. This is simple policework, tiresome but vital. The computer has done much of that for you, so make it count. Thanks."

Cyril collected his papers as people shuffled from the room. There was a definite buzz.

"I'm interviewing Cooper's neighbour, Ms Caroline Peet, later today. I'll brief you and add to the system." April smiled. "This shouldn't take too long and hopefully once the evidence is through either way regarding his demise, we can move on. Three deaths in quick succession must leave a trail. I also have an appointment with Ingrid Cooper. One after the other might prove interesting and informative."

Cyril said nothing. He had been involved in cases that were believed to be simple but they remained on the books unsolved. "Let's hope so, April, let's hope so!"

Chapter Thirteen

Owen's briefing was just that – brief. There had been the usual false sightings by officers and Owen was thankful that they had not opened it to the scrutiny of the general public; that often brought with it the usual crank calls, often from people purporting to be the youth.

"It has all the classic hallmarks of a youth off the rails and they can pinpoint the change in Martin," Shakti began. "There's even a rumour that he was collected by car not far from the school gate on more than one occasion. I've requested CCTV but from the pick-up location it would appear those in the car knew the area well enough to have the confidence that it was safe for them away from electronic eyes. Before you ask, they can't give dates only approximations so to run anything through ANPR would also be like finding an atom in space. What is relevant and useful, though, is the days he was not in school reference perfectly with the reports received of the youth in the garden and sightings on the railway. We can assume it was probably Martin."

DC Jones chipped in. "I chatted with a couple of his good mates with the Deputy Headteacher present. They too have seen a great change in him. He flashed a new mobile and he had some of those ear buds. Said his mum had won a bit of cash on the lottery. She hadn't and they didn't believe he was dealing drugs. That, I'm informed, takes place usually around the railway station and some of the passages that run through many of the housing estates. To quote the kids, 'The police don't seem to want to care.'"

"The fact is, if he doesn't come home this evening, we can assume he's being housed by whoever was collecting him. As the kids have no idea of the type of car, we're at a dead end." As Owen spoke, there was frustration in every word. "A dark blue or black four by four. That's it. But then one kid thought it might be a Hyundai but they couldn't be sure. So, Jones, check every one of those vehicles in that colour on the database, check the reg with ANPR in the Harrogate area so it can be crossed off the list. If he's not found in twenty-four hours it goes public. Radio, TV and social media. Get the News Media Team to draw up an appeal, Shakti. I want it ready to go local and nationwide."

***

Martin Dawson waited in the doorway of The Westminster Arcade. This was the quieter opening that led onto Union Street. It was not the most popular part of the shopping precinct. The last shop in the row had been empty for as long as he could remember. The arcade was a favourite of his mother's and the thought that she might appear made this rendezvous more threatening. He kept his hood up and his eyes fixed on the multistorey car park opposite. He blew out a sigh quickly checking the time on his phone and then comparing his watch; there was a difference of five minutes; he believed the phone. They were late as usual. Tapping his feet nervously, he slipped his hand towards his chest to feel for the small package he had secured within the zipped pocket. The large parcel had been switched successfully. Clockwork and child's play Star and the others had assured him. *Collect the first package. Wait. Swop that for a smaller package, wait. Deliver package. Job done.* He mimicked the words of the girl who had coached him. She had also said the job was eighty percent waiting, five percent excitement and the rest fear and she was right. But the rewards were worthwhile for the risks taken and more money was made than by doing anything else.

He paused as he watched a young couple approach. To avoid eye contact he turned to look in the empty shop window until they had sauntered past. Their laughter began to echo as they progressed deeper within the confines of the arcade.

Lights flashed to his right through the metal bars of the darkened car park. Martin's phone vibrated and his eyes focused on the metal bars that ran vertically across the large, open sides to the car park. The flashing lights, the signal, could not be missed. Checking Union Street, he walked down the hill before entering via the vehicular exit. Tugging on his hood as far as it would go was instinctive, as was keeping his face down to avoid the CCTV cameras.

The rear door of the Honda CRV opened and Martin climbed in. Before he had time to close it fully, the car was reversing until there was a sudden rhythmic bang on the roof. The car stopped as the girl who had recruited Martin slid into the rear seat next to him.

"Parking paid." She turned to look at Martin and grinned. "Okay, bro? Job done?"

Martin nodded whilst trying to locate his seat belt.

"You got it, I know, just being polite." She held out her hand as the Honda lurched left and right in the traffic before moving up towards Harrogate's bus station.

Slipping his hand into his jacket he removed the package, handed it over to Star and immediately felt his body relax. He turned to look out of the darkened window but focused on nothing. This is how it had been the last few times and probably would be for the next. Little was said. The girl flicked through the wedge of notes before slipping it back into the envelope and securing it deep within the rear pocket of the front seat.

"With us for a second night, Kestrel?" This was the name that he had been tagged with – no one seemed to use a real name. "A few beers and preparation for tomorrow. It will be a welcome to Wetherby. It's an easy pick-up, a cheeky one too, just over the motorway from the prison. Youth accommodation for the naughty boys." She leaned over and squeezed his thigh. "If you're going to play these games, then play right under their noses." She winked. "Anyway, let's not think about that. You're too good to get stopped, we're training you too well and besides, Star will look after you." She tapped her chest with an outstretched finger.

The name Star suited her. She seemed to sparkle with enthusiasm. He found her attractive and fun. Martin closed his eyes. If this was like the previous journey it would take forty minutes before they hit the Leeds ring road and once there, they had to pass through Chapeltown and onto Harehills. The driver seemed cautious, taking many of the side roads and then checking his mirror before doubling back.

The vehicle was not stolen, it was registered to a legitimate business and would not have issues with ANPR. Caution was their watchword for success and there was an awareness that one random check could lead to problems, particularly when carrying the youngsters. It was now known that the police were looking for the boy in the back.

Ashton Mount looked like many of the streets in the area, they all climbed steeply away from the main road like ribs attached to a spine. The street to either side was flanked by back-to-back, red brick homes, each having a small garden to the front of the property. Many were topped with an additional dormer extension perched on the roof and the majority had a satellite dish affixed to the façade. It was as if each owner had tried to outdo the other. It made Martin think of a visit to Jodrell Bank he had taken with school.

Martin stared at each house as the Honda climbed the hill before pulling up outside number 17. Many of the front doors in the row were covered with fixed metal grilles of differing designs but each serving the same purpose. Since his first visit, the area had not sat comfortably with him. It was as if each house was a castle, protecting the owner and his contents from some hidden enemy or threat. He had not seen this in Harrogate apart from on some of the shuttered shop fronts. Number 17 was no different.

Martin tried to open the car door but he could not. Star had no problem as she quickly slammed hers before jogging round the car and opening Martin's.

"Child locks. No offence." She grinned and tapped his shoulder reassuringly. "Come on!"

As on previous occasions the car left. Lifting a bunch of keys from the inside of her jacket, she removed the lanyard from around her neck and approached the lock on the metal grille.

***

Caroline Peet asked April for the second time if she would like a drink. She was clearly nervous.

"To be honest, Detective Inspector, I've never been formally interviewed by the police before so do excuse my apprehension." She paused. "That might be a lie. I was stopped once in the car for speeding but that doesn't count, I suppose it's not the same is it?" She moved a cushion from the settee and asked April to sit. "Cooper's death was a dreadful business. One day you're here and the next ..."

April was determined to make her questioning quick and to the point. "Time is of the essence, Ms Peet, so please don't be offended by this question. Did you have a liaison with Mr Cooper?"

The pause was palpable and Peet began to fidget and flush a little. "Yes, but I don't see what that's got to do with anything."

"Please tell all. It's important and I can assure you it's in confidence."

Although she was slow to answer, Peet soon explained the whole affair, how it had started when he had helped her fix a light switch. "Ingrid was still with him then but I don't believe I was the first and I certainly know I wasn't the last. When his wife went shopping or to visit friends, he'd pop round. There was no harm, we enjoyed each other's company. As I say, I know he had others too, I heard rumours. Bit of a bugger with the women but I could see why!" She raised her eyebrows and a smile brushed her lips briefly.

"You mentioned to my colleague, DC Misra, he had a number of female friends come to the house after his wife left. Were you and he still lovers?"

"No, we'd fallen out big style. I know I was the one he blamed for their separation as if he were the innocent party for goodness sake! He had the brass neck to say that I was vindictive and a gossip and had done it deliberately, blaming me for word getting back to her. I didn't forgive him after that cruelty. We didn't speak again."

"What was your profession, Ms Peet?" April had seen her name on the LEA list and the question was really unnecessary. She hoped there would be more to the link.

"I was a peripatetic music specialist. I not only taught music, I specialised in teaching the violin. I was based for some time at either the Harrogate or Ripon Teachers' Centres. There was the odd time I'd visit Northallerton but I was mainly local and worked in several schools. I knew Stan from my work as well as being his neighbour."

"Can you confirm when you started working in this LEA?"

"I worked within the Bradford Authority when I started my teaching career, then moved here in the late eighties and stayed until retirement. Before you ask, I've never been married. Lived with a few and that has taught me all I needed to know about the male of the species. They're like kids, great to have for a short time but you're always happy to hand them back. Let's just say I like to be the one in control."

April jotted the words down verbatim.

***

Martin was spread across the settee, a game controller in his hands and the Play Station Virtual Reality headset wrapped around his face. The room was silent apart from his enthusiastic self-encouragement and damning verbal anger of his imaginary enemy. It was clear he was enthralled and fully engrossed in some kind of battle. His whole body moved and jerked in staccato spasm-like actions, followed closely by another until he finally slumped onto the settee as if he had been shot from the sky and killed. The game was clearly lost. Virtual reality gaming equipment was something he had always wanted but his mother could neither afford it nor did she approve. He recalled her exact, strong words: "It encourages gratuitous violence and glorified killing and as long as you're under this roof it's not happening!" He shook his head. Here, in this new, strange world, it was immediately brought on request. Whatever he seemed to ask for, he got. He had also asked for pizza and he knew it would come, the correct size and ingredients. Removing his head set he smiled. It was hard developing his skills as a new combat pilot but he would succeed over time. The smell of the pizza drifted into the room and he immediately felt hungry. It made him think of his mother. *Why could she not just understand him, cut him some slack?* Looking at the headset in his hand … *why could she not just let him have his way for a change now he was older? Maybe he was better off here, maybe she did not love him like she once did. These friends understood. Maybe he should have listened to Star sooner.*

***

April looked at Peet. There was more to this relationship than she had first thought. She knew she would have to leave soon if she were to make her next appointment.

"Maybe I'll have that coffee after all, if the offer still stands."

Caroline stood and went into the kitchen. April followed.

"Lovely garden," April complimented as she looked through the patio doors. The lawn stretched away towards a beech hedge that partly concealed an ornate wooden shed and a greenhouse. Trees ran along the far boundary. The whole space looked well-ordered and organised.

"It never stops, the work in the garden that is, but I find it totally relaxing. Love my greenhouse too. I can often be found in there relaxing in a deckchair on those cold, clear, sunny winter days just reading. I acquired green fingers from my father." She handed April her coffee. "He was a botanist. Worked for many years for Bradford Parks and Gardens. Sometimes he was based at Peel Park but for most of his time he was at Cartwright Hall. That was his favourite. He used to tell me about the floral clock they planted and the extensive hothouses. Goodness, they produced some beautiful plants and shrubs. Exotics coming from all over the world could be seen in some of the public glasshouses, plants you'd not expect to see in an industrial city like Bradford. I remember as a child, some of the flowers and their colours and scents were divine. Not only did they grow items for planting out but they produced flowers and greenery for the floral displays used in the municipal buildings.

"In his later years he lived here with me until he passed away. He instructed me how to set out the garden as you see it and brought many of the shrubs and greenhouse plants as cuttings from Bradford. He planted some of those trees when I first moved here, unusual variety he said. He brought all his diaries, journals and botanical books here too and I keep promising myself that I'll read them one day but they're still in the loft. People think retirement must be full of endless days and be boring but I can assure you it's not. I don't know how I found time to work."

"I've heard that said many times," April added. "Travelling round the schools, did you meet or know either a Dr John Rigby or a Mr Paul Seex?" April sipped her coffee.

Caroline Peet laughed. "Paul Seex? Bloody hell, Sexy Seex, there's a name from the past. He left long since."

"You know him?"

"Knew him. Let's say that I knew him in another life." The laugh had transformed into a chuckle. She collected a biscuit tin from a cupboard and placed it on the table. "Please, help yourself and do sit, you're making me nervous. Seex, bloody hell! I used to see him at the Teachers' Centre in Harrogate. As a young single woman, you soon got to know those slightly older men with a roving eye. To be honest, he was a nice enough chap with me. Became headteacher of a school near Boroughbridge."

***

Martin finished the pizza and slipped back onto the settee.

The door opened and two men entered, one was of Asian extraction. Martin had not seen him before, the other he had met the previous day. Both were in their early twenties. They chatted briefly out of Martin's earshot.

"He needs testing. Star's not too sure about his ability to keep it together when trouble appears." He turned to look at Martin who was back behind the Play Station goggles.

"Thought you told me he was fine on the last occasion?"

"Home ground, knew it well. Let's see how he copes on the next, it's a dummy run so if it goes tits up we'll know."

They took a seat opposite Martin. One tapped his leg

and Martin quickly removed the headgear, rubbed his eyes and smiled at the men facing him. He was immediately impressed by the clothes they wore. Their trainers were expensive and immaculate. Martin swung his feet from the settee looking at his own shoes; they were no match.

"I'm not going to introduce you two, other than to let you know this is Tea, as in the drink and not the letter. He's my boss and I guess yours too now."

Tea smiled and threw out his hand. Martin took it weakly, uncertain as to whether he should shake it firmly like his dad used to tell him to when he was little. There was something about the man's expression that brought a flutter of fear to his stomach. He looked hard and cold.

"I want you to know we're pleased that you've joined the group and your work is very much appreciated. To show our gratitude I have a small gift for you." He pulled out an envelope and tossed it to Martin. "You can look."

There was a wad of a hundred pounds in five-pound notes. "The games' console is yours, and I believe you have some trainers on order."

Martin nodded as he looked at the money.

"They're my gift also. There's always more to be had but we need you to be at home, more of an undercover operative where the police are not looking for you. It will be better for you as well as for us if you were at school and amongst your friends. Look on it as the next stage of your training. Star will be your link. She likes you, I know that, she told me. All of this," he pointed to the headset, "can stay at hers and she'll give you her details later. You'd be welcome there, she's a mate. When you're older you'll be your own man. For now, you'll get the jobs in the times you're out of school. There'll be others too, a different skill. More danger, a bit like that but more real." He pointed to the computer.

Martin looked at the headset and then back at Tea.

"This is how you do it."

The explanation was straightforward. On their leaving, Star came in carrying some beers. She handed him one. "Think about it tonight. Now let's just go over what we're expecting of you tomorrow." She opened the laptop and brought up Google Earth.

Chapter Fourteen

Cyril had received the initial, abbreviated autopsy findings for Cooper including the toxicology results. As suspected, he had been poisoned but yet again by the use of another plant-based toxin – Taxine alkaloids derived from – *Taxus baccata*, the Common Yew. He picked up the phone and dialled Julie's mobile number whilst continuing to speed read the report. It went immediately to answerphone. He did not leave a message, he read:

Serum samples show taxine type B alkaloids in the blood and confirmed by the Royal Botanical gardens to be from the Common Yew. There was no evidence of needles within the gastrointestinal tract. We are assuming until more finite tests are carried out that the toxin was administered in a purer form. Still consumed, possibly from the flask. We can assume the digoxin reading was a false positive owing to the toxin being similar to digitalis. Considering the concentration of the dose, death would quickly follow an arrhythmia resulting in a severe cardiogenic shock. As previously noted, the initial autopsy showed evidence of congestion of the brain and lungs where alveolar haemorrhage was present, but apart from dilation to the right chamber of the heart, no major issues were noted in the heart itself.

April had tagged a hand written note beneath – *Common yew has been used as an abortifacient and for assassination! The plot thickens!!*

***

April arrived at Ingrid Cooper's house later than expected. The welcome had been cold but civil. April had been surprised at Caroline Peet's open and frank discussion and wanted to gain as much information as she could while she was co-operative. She had made a note to check on the employment history of Caroline Peet's father to confirm what she had been told.

"There's nothing to discuss. I'm saddened by Stan's death, obviously. You can't love someone, marry them, set up home and have life plans without having some emotional connection, but that link, those feelings might not be what you or others expect of you. If I were to be honest with you, there were times when I could have happily murdered him myself. He could be an absolute bastard I can tell you."

April knew Ingrid had seemed surprised when she was told there was a possibility that her ex-husband's death might not have been through natural causes nor an accident. This could not be seen in her expression. She was in total control of her feelings but she was still amazed she would use the term *murder*.

"Detective Inspector you said?"

"Yes, Richmond."

"So, you believe he was killed, murdered? Well, Detective Inspector Richmond, he enjoyed all of the things in life beginning with the letter 'F'. Fun, fishing, fellowship, fornicating, flirting, particularly flirting with anything young and pretty. Funny thing about Stan, he was a total stranger to fidelity. I could have happily strangled Peet, that bitch of a neighbour, but in some ways, I came to realise she did me a favour and I found someone more mature with a broader vocabulary and more loving in the true sense of the word but you will know that, of course, you'll have checked?"

"That's two people you would happily have murdered." April raised an eyebrow. "As you've just demonstrated, to murder someone, you have to have a strong motive. Do you know anyone who might want to see him dead?"

Ingrid could not hold back the laugh. "I'm nervous and I seem to have a short fuse! I'm sorry. I see why you ask me that. I was joking about … never mind. It's a number of years since we lived in the same house. I didn't know what he was doing or who he was meeting so I'm damned if I'd have an inkling now about his life and his loves. Remember, Inspector, if you consider alliteration acceptable, philandering could have been one of his words as it sounds as though it might fit with the list. Of course that behaviour makes enemies by the very nature of the act. Whether that's a strong enough motive to commit murder I couldn't say, but crimes of passion have been with us since the first man. All I can assume, considering that thought, is there might be many husbands or wives waiting for the opportunity to get even unless he'd changed over the last years and old age eventually weakened the lead in his pencil!"

That mental picture brought a pause in the interview as April worked to re-establish her train of thought.

"Considering the list of 'F' words, what about fragility?"

"How very perceptive of you. As a woman, you'll know

121

that all men are fragile creatures and need their egos stroking and boosting on a daily basis. That's my experience anyway and he was no different, probably more so than the rest. He needed the constant attention of others, the praise, the promotion, the promiscuity and the power – Frankly, in my opinion, he was a prick!"

April sensed real venom within the closing statement.

"You might be aware that two of his colleagues, Paul Seex and Dr John Rigby have also been murdered. They worked within the Authority at the same time."

Ingrid brought a hand to her mouth and it was clear from her facial expression the news had come as a shock.

"Seex and then Rigby. But I can't say more. You knew them?" April watched her carefully, knowing it was not always what someone said but how they reacted to the question and their response using nonverbal clues.

"Stan's colleagues. He used to call them his partners in crime, the Brat Pack."

"Just the three?" April asked, feeling for the first time she might have a lead.

"No, there were others, two maybe three more but the names escape me. Murdered too?"

April shook her head. "We need those names."

***

Although it was late, April hoped Cyril would still be working as the various caseloads needed careful co-ordination. He was and Owen was with him. She tapped on the door to his office and entered. There was a skip in her step.

"A possible breakthrough and a point worth noting, Peet has a history and maybe a working knowledge of exotic plants. Her father was a specialist gardener all of his life."

Cyril sat back. "Are we checking?"

"There's more, sir, we have more potential victims." She explained the course of her afternoon's work.

"Names?" Cyril asked. There was an immediate enthusiasm in the question but it was quickly dampened.

"Not yet. She can't remember but is optimistic they'll come to her. I've invited her to come in and look at the LEA lists in the hope it will jog her memory."

"Great! Let's hope that something might come of this. Speaking of lists, we have a number of people linked to the Facebook Page, Rigby's reunion group. The techies have managed to work their magic with their Satanic wizardry and yielded mysteries."

Owen chuckled. "When you move with the times all manner of secrets will be revealed."

"Right, if you say so! Anyway, April, you might use that list first. Admin, according to this, is done by a Barbara Burton." Cyril looked at her and then back at Owen. "You said she didn't keep a track of her ex, Stan Cooper? If that was the case then I wonder why she was a friend of the group?" He turned back to April. "Maybe when she's in here you might ask her."

"Bloody hell," April whispered, "that was not what I was expecting."

***

Melanie Masters faced Norma Halsall. They sat at an outside table overlooking the Mercer Art Gallery. Although the sunshine broke through the clouds only occasionally, the weather was surprisingly warm. They had ordered sandwiches and a bowl of fries. Each nursed a large glass of red wine. The news now breaking of Cooper's death had brought fresh speculation. Norma, who seemed to be the fount of all knowledge or at least the web gossip, had laughed somewhat callously as she mentioned the demise of those she referred to as the three musketeers. She was, however, now considering whether the killings would continue and would swiftly turn into the possible destruction of a dirty dozen.

Melanie, her mouth full of wine, had nearly sprayed the contents over the table and it was only by her swift hand action that she saved the day. She coughed and choked slightly as she managed to swallow the wine.

"Rigby was a handsome yet lecherous sod – but Seex?" Melanie commented, remembering more than one incident.

"Insidious, weasel of a man. I could never trust him and from what people said he was tarred with the same brush as Rigby. I remember one time when he offered me a lift home, after a union meeting, I think it was. I wasn't married then and I'm not sure about him. Bloody hell, I kid you not, he pulled over just off Franklin Road, near the cemetery. You know how dark it is along there. There were no pleasantries on his part, just an expectation. It was like fighting off an octopus!"

"And?" Melanie leaned forward hoping to hear of some public tryst.

"He got short bloody shrift and a few choice words I can tell you. Do you know what he said?"

Melanie did not sip any wine not knowing what her friend was about to divulge and shook her head.

"'If you co-operate with me, I'll be able to help you with your future career.' Those were his exact words. I'd just put in for a scale post and he knew it. If he could have his way, have a quick shag, then he could guarantee that I'd move up in the world."

The waiter brought their order.

"When you think of what went on behind closed doors then people wouldn't believe you." Norma tutted as if disgusted but she could not keep the giggle from betraying her true feelings.

"It goes on now. People are just a little more subtle. Look at office parties when wine flows and inhibitions disappear." Melanie picked a fry from the bowl and nibbled at it. "It's just people, being people. It's not done for personal or professional gain, there are no false promises made and I guess neither are they expected. The usual end result is that of regret and embarrassment. I've been there on a few occasions so I know the difference. Society, Norma, was different back then as was the teaching profession."

Norma finished the last bite of her sandwich. "So, as I see it, considering their ages, they must have pissed someone off pretty badly for them to be selected for an early dispatch."

"Never get angry, just even is what you're insinuating. You're a hard woman. But I see your point. There will come a time when we all have an opportunity to even old scores. Surely it crossed your mind sitting in that car in Franklin Road?"

"No, if I'm honest, a swift knee in the testicles might be appropriate but certainly not murder! He behaved badly but I was a big girl and I could handle the man. In some ways I was flattered and who knows what might have taken place if I'd liked him? I would probably have taken full advantage of the situation but as I said, he was a weasel. He had one of those pointy faces. My mother always told me to try before I buy … I tried a lot." She winked and finished her wine. "I can't be doing with all these modern types who are insulted by an innocent wolf whistle. Bloody snowflakes, the lot of them!"

Chapter Fifteen

Martin sat in the back of the Honda. The headphones blotted out any sound. He was agitated and he clenched his hands together going over the instructions he had received the previous evening. He had been assured it would be straightforward and he had no reason to doubt Star's word, after all he trusted her. As she had said, it was just a pick up, drop off and collect – a swop. He had been to Wetherby before but only with his mother shopping. He was nervous.

The pick-up moved into the inside lane of the north bound A1M. The passenger was engrossed in a paperback. The pages had been curled at the top corner. His feet were positioned on the dashboard. The rhythmic flicks of the wipers were in some ways therapeutic. The rain was an unnecessary distraction but it could work in their favour.

"If we stop quickly your beautiful size nine trainers will be pushed where your teeth are, you know that don't you? Something to do with an exploding airbag. Your feet shouldn't be there." The driver turned to look at his passenger but he was too engrossed in the book. "About five minutes and we'll be having our usual mechanical problem." He nudged the passenger. "Are you listening? Four minutes. Get your arse in gear. The spray from the passing cars and poor visibility will help but you might get a tad wet – shame!"

The passenger said nothing just took hold of the corner

of the page and roughly folded it over before tossing the book onto the dashboard. He retracted his feet and collected the shoebox-sized package from the footwell. It was heavily wrapped against the weather.

The Honda moved slowly along Freemans Way, a road within a housing estate that looped as it approached the A168 that ran parallel with the A1M. At the loop in the road was a public garden. A wooden pergola was situated within the fencing and the footpath ran from the road and garden to the right, taking pedestrians and cyclists below the two roads in a concrete, tube-like underpass. It then became part of the Wetherby Railway Path before appearing at the far side of the motorway next to Wetherby Racecourse and the open countryside.

A drop off had been attempted on a previous occasion. It involved stopping at the spot whilst travelling south. The package had been dropped from the motorway bridge onto the pathway below, but it was believed that it could never be predicted who might be beneath or approaching the tunnel exit. It was too insecure. The way it was now planned proved to be better. This was the third successful drop at this location and it was decided it would be the last for some time. Regularity in the drug game was for the foolhardy. Considering all of the possible drop places in the area, there was no need for carelessness.

The pick-up began to slow. "Don't forget. Just after the sign is the gate in the perimeter fencing."

The electronic motorway sign jutted out over the hard shoulder like one wing of the Angel of the North. Checking the rear-view mirror, the driver continued to slow the vehicle. His finger moved to hover over the hazard warning light button. He pressed it before driving onto the hard shoulder, travelling under the sign before pulling up by the barrier. The gate was immediately to his left. The passenger flipped up his jacket hood, exited and went to examine the rear tyre, an excuse that enabled him to scan down the motorway. The spray from the constant stream of passing vehicles made identifying those approaching impossible and there was always an element of risk that a passing police or Highways Agency vehicle might appear and jeopardise the drop. In the event of this occurring, to feign breakdown the cab had been fitted with a switch that would not allow the engine to start. A flick would see it righted and all would be well. Satisfied with the risk, he collected the package, flipped over the steel barrier and tucked it round the other side of the gate that was intentionally left ajar. It was placed in the deep grass. Within a minute the paperback was opened and the pick-up was pulling away, disappearing into the rain.

As instructed, Martin left the Honda and walked down towards the tunnel-like underpass, before running up the grass bank to its concrete edge. He quickly climbed the fence. Once on top, he scanned the motorway perimeter fencing and focused on the electronic gantry positioned away to his right and over the motorway. Spotting the gate, his target, he jumped off the fence and ran across the A168, collecting the package before retracing his steps. It was bigger than the last one. He popped the package down and grabbed the top of the first fence. To his relief, the pergola and garden area was empty of people. He dropped back down, tossed the package over and quickly followed. Remembering his instructions, he turned under the road and followed the graffiti defaced tunnel. He now had a long walk. The rain grew stronger and he tried to tuck the package inside his coat but with little success. Ahead he saw a cyclist. The bike was upside down leaning against the hedge and the Lycra-clad figure was attempting to replace the rear wheel back onto the bike. Martin was unsure as to what he should do. He tugged at his hood and moved more quickly. The cyclist turned.

"Can you do us a favour please and just hold the bike whilst I get this wheel back on? The gears make life difficult." The request came with a smile and Martin saw the rainwater drip from the man's chin. Star's instructions came to him: *whatever you do, act respectfully and as normal as possible.* Martin moved closer and popped the packet on the ground.

The cyclist nodded. "Thanks. It'll take but a few minutes."

***

Cyril had noted April's suspicions regarding Peet and her father and had delegated the task of investigating them further to one of the team.

Detective Constable Stuart Park finalised his investigation of Edward Peet. As his daughter, Caroline, had correctly pointed out, he had worked for Bradford Parks and Gardens and had an unblemished record. She had failed to add that his speciality was trees and he was a qualified arborist. He had checked the meaning of the qualification. For some strange reason he also researched his name in the Public Records for deaths and the information was forthcoming. His death corresponded with Peet's statement. Already late, Stuart Park glanced at his watch before adding the information to the system and tagging a note on the board in the Incident Room before he left for home.

***

"Appreciate your help. Thanks. Pete, my name's Pete." The cyclist held out his hand.

"Marti ..." he stopped himself midword. "No problem. Must get on. Didn't expect so much rain." His voice was shaky as he bent to collect the package. Moving away he raised his hand in a wave. Once he felt at a safe distance, he turned to look back at Pete. Relieved, he saw him turning the bike onto its wheels. He did not, however, see him remove his helmet and stop the helmet cam from recording.

Within five minutes Martin checked the back of his hand and the name, Walton Road. His next meeting point had been scribbled in ink, fearful he would forget. From what he remembered of the Street View images, it was remote and crossed the cycle path much further down. He could hear the odd car or wagon but could not see the road from his present position. According to his instructions he must wait there. He started to jog, tucking the package firmly beneath his right arm. On arrival he took a deep breath and paused just away from the crossroads.

Pete, the cyclist, removed his mobile. "I've spotted Martin Dawson, the missing Harrogate lad. I'm sending images through from my helmet cam. Can't a man have a day off work?" Pete Cosgrove would normally be driving a traffic police vehicle had it not been his rest day. Transferring the file onto his mobile he sent it giving a description of the direction in which the lad was travelling.

The distant roar of a motorbike, the engine note raw and shrill, was growing from Martin's left-hand side. He looked up the wet tarmac track but it soon disappeared as the road rounded a bend and yet the discordant noise continued to grow from that direction. Martin had been brought up with bikes and he assessed it was a mini moto type dirt bike. His father had always ridden powerful machines.

He remembered the day he heard of his father's death and the state of his mum when she received the news. He had been in bed when the knock broke the morning silence and police officers came into the house. His mum knew there was something wrong and she went down on her knees. He could see it as if it were only yesterday. He discovered that a car had pulled out of a side road on that dark morning when Dad was travelling to work. He had not died immediately but was on life support until the family agreed to turn it off. Although young, he could never forget. He had ridden pillion with his father many times, often fast, sweeping round bends as if on rails and he had loved every minute whilst encouraging his dad to go faster. They had watched the bike races on television and talked about visiting the TT and the road races in Ireland one day when he was older. Like his father, Martin's hero was John McGuinness. Now, however, he was frightened of any kind of motorbike. On seeing the bike appear he realised that he had been correct as to the type and he moved back towards the hedge.

The bike screamed towards him. The rider's hair and open jacket blew and flapped demonically as he stood on the pegs, catching all the wind and rain, before sliding the rear of the bike to a halt just by Martin's feet.

"Get on!" the rider screamed. "Now! Get on this bloody bike, now!"

Martin was frozen to the spot. He stared at the machine as he held the package. Steam rose in wisps from the hot exhaust. He tried to step further away but he was against the hedge.

"Get on the bike!"

As if rooted to the spot he could not move. The scream of the revving engine filled his ears and mind as if mesmerising and paralysing his very being. He could see his father, wires and tubes seeming to be protruding from every facial orifice. Martin held out the package and shook his head. The rider, losing patience, reached and snatched the offering, stuffed it into his jacket, zipped it up and sped across the main road without looking. The pitch of the engine screamed as if to torment Martin further. Thoughts of his dad remained. He could see nothing else. He felt his bottom lip quiver and a tear appeared on his cheek. Slowly his mind cleared and fear tumbled in the pit of his stomach. He realised he was now without the package he should have received in exchange. He had nothing. He had failed. The noise of the bike had long since died in direct contrast to his increasing panic and fear. His self-pity, however, did not last long as the sound of a siren could be heard somewhere in the distance. It was growing louder.

Chapter Sixteen

Barbara Burton chuckled to herself. "Yes, I'm one of two administrators of the private Facebook page, *Pedagogues' Place*. I made up the title. Some might say it's a little gauche but then one has to consider what people's reactions might be. Believe me, young lady, after thirty-odd years in a classroom you learn to switch off from the suggestions, criticisms and the advice we're all bombarded with these days by the faceless keyboard warriors. We had our fair share of the 'so-called experts'." She made the inverted comma marks in the air with her fingers as she slowed her speech to emphasise the point. "What with HMI, the Ofsted teams, advisors and the parents – yes, Detective Constable Misra, even the parents thought themselves the real experts and on many occasions were beyond reproach. Remember this, I learned it throughout my long career, everyone's an expert when it comes to education and schools because everyone's been through the system. You may well have said this yourself at some point. 'It's not right what schools do today. It was never like that when I was there.' And the best. 'They'd never do that if I were in charge of a classroom.' That's my favourite. Reflective expertise I call it. Bullshit might be the better and more accurate terminology. Anyway, I'll put away the old soapbox. How can I help you?"

"The Facebook page?" Shakti hinted respectfully.

"Right, yes. Some of us were members of the U3A, and this group, of which we now speak, was started as an offshoot of that; made up of people we knew in our working careers. We wanted to meet for chats and get togethers to see how well life was treating us or not as the case might be. We wanted to help each other and on occasion, to chew the fat. We never referred to the meetings as reunions, I mean, as it wasn't a term we liked. Do you have them, reunions in the force?"

Shakti shook her head. She had popped a Dictaphone on the table between them. "No time for that and besides, not been in the force long enough. It was kind of you to see me. I'm sorry for the tragic loss of your former teaching friends."

"Strangely, they were not all friends but we were in the same profession. Some remained true to their calling and worked diligently as teachers, whilst others climbed the slippery pole of promotion to reach positions of power." Barbara Burton screwed up her face to show a degree of displeasure.

"How many members do you have?"

"Thirty-seven if we still count … yes well. Remember, this was never going to be an expanding group, owing to time's onward march it was always going to end in zero. We'd have a last man standing or woman to be politically correct! Unless, of course, we change the membership criteria. You had to have been working within the LEA between 1980 and 2000. Now you'd think we'd have hundreds of willing participants but many have moved away from the area and some have a certain degree of apathy in revisiting old times and let's not forget some have passed on. Reminiscing is not for the faint-hearted. One of our members believes if you look back for too long you crash into a tree. She has a point but I like to think it's where we wrinklies turn up old and find our youth again if only for an hour or so. My glass is always half-full."

Shakti had a list of questions but if Barbara continued to answer every one as if she were giving a class lecture, she would be there all day. "Can you tell me about your last get together, names of those present and if you chatted with any of the deceased?"

"That would be about four weeks ago, yes. I have the exact date; I'll get it for you in a tick. I booked a room at the Wayfarers, just off Parliament Street. They supplied the food. Good it was too. We had about fifteen present and the three boys came, the deceased, I should say. I chatted to them all during the meeting. Two had not been well but they had all finished their professional careers on grounds of ill health, so that's not surprising. However, what was surprising, now I come to think of it, was the number of members who contacted me afterwards to say they'd been quite unwell. Suffered from *Gandhi's revenge*." Barbara paused as she saw Shakti's expression change. "Maybe I carelessly used the wrong term considering your ethnicity, my apologies. Food poisoning, dear. What was also strange, and it's really only just come back to me now on reflection, we'd suffered a similar problem at the previous venue and that's why we went to the Wayfarers. Never put those two things together until just now. Sickness and diarrhoea. I believe Paul Seex was quite poorly with it."

"Who else was ill?" Shakti felt a frisson of excitement build as she posed the question and witnessed a sudden realisation strike Barbara.

There was a long pause as Barbara understood the implications of what she was saying.

"The three who have since passed away were ill after both occasions. My goodness, you don't believe I've inadvertently put them in harm's way, do you?"

Shakti saw real concern in Barbara's face. "No, this can happen and does happen regularly. Food hygiene is key to any establishment preparing and serving the food. You only booked the venue, you didn't prepare the food."

Barbara visibly relaxed.

"You mentioned others too?"

"Yes, yes. Christopher Foster, he was an advisory teacher for a few years. Now he didn't come to this event but I remember his wife telling me he was quite ill after the previous do. And then there was Colin Drummond, not a nice man when he was younger and I'm sad to say he didn't mellow. Arrogant and obnoxious. Thought he was brighter and better than the rest. Bit of a Lothario, our Drummond. Let's just say you never wanted to be visiting the store cupboard when he was in – mind, now, his wife keeps him under a tight rein. He too was very poorly."

"You've only given me men's names. What about the ladies present on these occasions?"

There was another silence as if a penny were falling a long distance. "Do you know what, young lady?"

Shakti leaned forward in eager anticipation her head shaking slightly. "What?"

"Now I come to think of it I never received one complaint from the ladies. Yes, I recall some saying that they'd eaten the same as their partners but they had no symptoms. How strange is that? I certainly ate my fair share and I was fine after both."

"How is the food served at these gatherings?"

"It's a buffet. We help ourselves."

"And the drinks?"

"Some buy for others and others buy their own. It's never wise to get into buying rounds with the men. Some of the chaps can consume alcohol as if it's about to go on ration. Mind, to be fair, some of the girls can polish off the odd gin in rapid fire! I recall that certain wives go to the buffet for their husbands. Strangely, Ingrid, Stan Cooper's ex-wife, went for his. I thought that very kind-spirited considering the way he had always treated her."

"And the time before that?" Shakti was hoping beyond all hope she would tell her that she did the same.

"No, I don't think so but I can't be sure. If it had been me, I'd have slipped a Mickey Finn either into his pint or his sandwich for all the womanising he did, that's if you can put a Mickey in food." She looked at the police officer opposite, her eyebrows raised hoping for an answer. She quickly realised what she had in fact implied before blurting out. "Oh dear! Sorry. I can assure you I did nothing of the sort."

Shakti closed the interview, collected the dates and a list of members' names to check against those found after Rigby's laptop was investigated and thanked her.

"If anything else should come to mind I'd be grateful for a call." She handed her a card containing her number. "This is the fastest way to contact me. You won't reach me directly but Control will put you straight through."

***

Relieved his mother and siblings were not at home, Martin

removed the key from the store that was bolted to the rear wall of the house and let himself in. Opening the fridge, he took out some orange cordial before flicking the kettle switch. He was soaked through and still felt cold even after the taxi journey.

Once he had calmed down, he knew the one place he needed to be was here at home. What would they do when he failed to deliver the package, either package? The thought of Star's expression or the reactions of the other two if he were to turn up empty-handed did not bear contemplating. He paused and thought about his leaving the scene. It seemed so surreal now he was in his own kitchen. Playing the journey back in his mind, he could scarcely believe what he had done.

On hearing the approaching siren, Martin had turned up Moor Lane, in the direction from which he had first seen the motorbike, before hiding in a small copse set just back from the road. The siren had grown louder and he could see the blue of the strobe lights. It did not stay long and soon disappeared slowly along the road. He waited thirty minutes feeling the spot was secure from anyone looking for him. He turned off the phone they had given to him believing it might be tracked but then, in panic, he stamped on it a number of times before scattering the pieces in the field as far as he could throw them. His own phone he kept safe but switched off.

The drizzle continued but it was of no consequence; fear and the need to run had blocked the worry of getting soaked. He wore nothing they had given to him but he still rummaged through his pockets. There was the envelope containing the hundred pounds. He checked to see if they had placed anything else within but there was nothing other than the money.

Checking the road in both directions he set off away from the cycle path before taking a well-used farm track. After five minutes he was on the outer road of Wetherby Races. It was eerily quiet. One way was clearly barred so he began to jog in the opposite direction. He felt so exposed. The road seemed private. No traffic flowed. Within minutes he was at a roundabout and a sign showing that he was on the outskirts of Wetherby. The thin veils of fine drizzle continued to fall. He could not stop, he needed to continue even if he were exposed. He had no alternative but to take a risk. He needed to get home. He jogged along the grass verge on the edge of York Road keeping his head down.

Within minutes the prison appeared to his right and to his relief the preparations he had made with Star came flooding back. The Google Map was clear in his head and he knew that he would soon cross the motorway and then be in Wetherby centre. He needed to get to the supermarket, the one he had been to with his mother. They had a free phone after the checkouts where you could call a taxi. Before that, however, he needed a change of appearance. He needed a coat.

Within the hour he had been dropped not far from home. The taxi money was well spent. For the first time since leaving the Honda he relaxed. In another half hour the nerves would return. He had to face his mother.

Pouring the boiling water onto the cordial released the sweet smell of orange and he lowered his face to allow it to fill his nostrils; a reassuring aroma that helped him relax. It was now just a case of waiting for the wrath to descend. It would be a different anger than that he would have received from the others in Leeds as this would come from someone who truly loved and cared for him. He took a pen from the kitchen drawer and collected a piece of paper. He wrote a simple note in block capitals and attached it to the fridge using one of the magnets his mother had collected over the years.

***

April was by her desk when Shakti returned.

"You need to hear this. How someone hasn't put two and two together from the group and called us I can't understand. You're going to be amazed."

April sat as she played the Dictaphone. Two other officers moved closer after April had beckoned them. Shakti said nothing but folded her arms as she leaned against the edge of a desk and looked at each colleague in turn as they listened.

"We need to speak with each and every one from this last meeting and the previous meetings." April handed back the Dictaphone. "Everyone, Shak, including those who said they were ill after their visit. What better way to hide any malpractice than by being a victim yourself? We need to eliminate as many from the search as possible. Some have unfortunately been naturally eliminated and those are all men."

Shakti left immediately and started collating names with addresses and contact numbers. She also tagged science and chemistry expertise to the equation. For the first time she felt as though they were getting closer to finding the answer.

Chapter Seventeen

Cyril swivelled on his chair as he sat back, his feet resting on the upturned waste bin. His phone was on speaker as he listened to Caner's latest findings whilst allowing the tip of his electronic cigarette to roll along his bottom lip. Since marrying he had been determined to kick the habit even though he had protested to Julie that he was only producing steam. Her retort had been unhelpful and rude but it brought a smile which is more than could be said when receiving a personal call from Caner.

"Further tests, Cyril, I'm pleased to say, give us an even better insight into what we, or should I say you, are dealing with. Poison is such an ancient art. It's how the toxin is produced and administered that brings the real conundrums and the need for quality scientific analysis. As you now know, Cyril, these poisons are all plant derivatives and relatively common plants at that. This is not a spur of the moment action we are investigating. These deaths have been well-planned. Why do I say this?" He did not wait for a reply and if he had he would have paused for a while. "The toxicity of plants is various as to their growing season. Some, however, maintain their potency throughout the year with only slight variation in their efficacy, whilst others can fluctuate broadly. So, we can presume from that the person extracting the poisons has a good working understanding of horticulture. Possibly expertise."

After deeply inhaling his electronic cigarette, Cyril interrupted whilst trying to blow a smoke ring from the vapour. "Surely you just go to any search engine and it spits out the relevant information you need."

There was an audible tutting and Cyril could imagine Caner shaking his head in the belief he was discussing facts of a subtle scientific nature with an imbecile. "That's all very well but there are nuances that would need to be more fully understood. Besides, most of what you find on the web is not as accurate as people believe. You're an intelligent man, Cyril, and you're aware of that more than most ..."

"So, what do you have?" Failing to make a ring and then Caner's patronising tone proved to be the last straws.

"Crystallisation, Cyril. Our killer, I believe, has concentrated the extraction of the toxin to such a degree within a crystalline format."

"Like Crystal Meth?" Cyril asked in swift response as he immediately sat up. Things were beginning to sound more interesting.

"Sorry, no. Meth is made using amphetamines and is not derived in any way from plants. It's purely chemical in its formation and that process incorporates many dangerous substances and actions. People can be seriously hurt in the manufacturing process. Ask Julie to explain over dinner. Your killer has some sort of scientific or chemical background, they can get hold of chemicals required for this specific manufacture and they have the wherewithall to control and administer the doses. I can only speculate on that at present but will look into it further and get back to you. We're not talking the sophisticated chemicals that come under registration." Caner paused.

"Does that mean the poisons produced can be administered through the consumption of food or drink and not separately in isolation?"

"Indeed, they can. It's what we've identified from Rigby's PM that we note the immediate application of the poison. It was put directly into the bloodstream through an open wound. That poison was sufficient and the self-application had to be cleverly planned. I believe those killed knew their murderer well, possibly trusted them. Thought you should know as soon as the latest Forensic findings came in. Must dash. A pleasure as always. I'll let you have a list of the basics, let's say the domestic shed science and the chemistry lesson needed to complete the extraction process, as soon as."

The line went dead and Cyril's finger pressed to end the call before he moved through to the Incident Room. He needed to see who was teaching chemistry from the lists and then he must leave the station. He had planned to surprise Julie and drive her to The White Bear in Masham for an early evening meal and, if the weather was fine, a stroll through the town. He had booked it a few days before and arranged to collect the old Bentley, the car left to him by his father, and stored at Julie's parents' home. Checking his watch, he needed to do it in the next hour and leave before three that afternoon.

***

DS Dan Grimshaw sat opposite DC Brian Smirthwaite as they considered the Forensic evidence detailing the cycle track and footprints found around the area of Cooper's parked Volvo on the day of his death. It was clearly a type of training shoe with a specific pattern to the sole, and stylised with an 'S', a size seven.

Grimshaw held the photographs and read the accompanying notes. "From the National Footwear Reference Collection. That's a small man or a large lady. Forty in European size and that's visible on the impression. They believe they're relatively new with some wear to the right heel. Skechers, according to the report and we have a possible weight of the suspect. According to the database, *Treadmate*, the reference for tyre tread patterns held by the police nationally, the cycle tyre is from a hybrid, go anywhere type bicycle. It's suggested here the bike was not ridden but pushed owing to the grass compression and the depth of indentation. You have to hand it to them, bloody clever these people"

"According to the report, there's no evidence to suggest whether the marks were made on that day …" Smirthwaite scanned the report, his finger guiding his reading as he worked through the page. "Yep, here. Weather for the twenty-four hours either side of the discovery. The light rain, the day before, was a contributory factor in the markings being so clear. The same imprints were found close to where Cooper left the fishing tackle on the bank. That, my friend, is who we're looking for." He tapped the shoe print.

"Has anyone thought that if this person is female and considering our Mr Cooper's reputation, it could have been a rendezvous? Possible alfresco sex? It's just a thought." Grimshaw did not sound convinced with his own theory and shook his head. "Do people have alfresco sex at that age? Forget that. Make sure that this information's distributed. The bike and the shoe size will be critical."

***

April drove towards Killinghall along Otley Road having arranged to see Rigby's ex-wife. The name Killinghall seemed appropriate considering the investigation and it was the first time she had reflected on the name in all the time she had been in Harrogate.

The afternoon sun was warm and it made a change from the earlier grey and constant drizzle. Pulling up outside the building that once was the old parish rooms, she parked and checked the address. Within minutes she was at the front door. The house was the end stone cottage of a row of five. A dark green Virginia Creeper clung overenthusiastically to much of the building's façade and was in the process of blindfolding the cottage as it had now covered the outer edges of the windows.

On hearing the click of a gate set within a stone arch to her right, she turned and moved towards the sound, approaching the corner of the building just as a face appeared from the side of the house gable. Both were suddenly surprised. They stopped.

"Oh! Goodness, sorry. DI Richmond?" The voice was confident and accompanied by a smile. "That was a bit of a surprise!"

"Yes, sorry to startle you." April held out her ID. "Thank you for seeing me."

"Come this way. I'm making the most of this welcome afternoon sunshine. I didn't expect it after such a poor morning."

April followed. Like the front of the house there was an air of neglect around the whole property. It was clear that there had not long since been a formality to the house and the garden area but that was gradually being lost, nature was beginning to rebel against the enforced structure and order. Even following her hostess, April could see the same there. Joan Rigby's hair was long and unkempt and her clothes, although not in any way shabby, seemed tired. A dog barked from inside, a shallow yap, that of a small dog.

"That's Trixie, I've left her in as she's too fussy. We'd get nothing done. Do excuse the garden, it's not what it was or what I'd like it to be, but old age and poverty take their toll. Besides, the butterflies and bees like it and in many ways, I do too. It got me down at first but I quickly learned to fight those feelings. I do what I can. I've put some chairs out. How can I help? I've not seen John for a long time. I was, however, saddened by his death. Funny, when we split, I'd have happily danced on his grave but I think time is, as is often said, a healer of most things. Then there's the others too. Murder, I believe. You don't expect it, not here, not in Harrogate. May I offer you some tea? I have this cold herbal drink." She pointed to her glass.

April held up her hand. "No, thank you. I don't want to take too much of your time. Did you know Seex and Cooper?"

"To be honest I'd forgotten all about them until this. I'd made a life of my own. At first, Ian, our son, was very supportive but he has his own life to live. I make no demands and I see very little of him really. I'd like more time with him but what mother wouldn't? It really did affect him. I sometimes think we parents cause more harm than good as far as our offspring are concerned and I believe one day we will reap what we sow. John was very dedicated to his work. If he wasn't actually there, he was at home talking about it. For him it was his life, a true vocation or so I

147

thought. Let's just say some of the enthusiasm for the profession was for his own personal gratification, hence the split. Do you believe, Inspector, that his past might just have caught up with him?"

April's eyes fell on the greenhouse, it too had seen better days. "That's what we are trying to find out. Is there anyone who might have wanted to seek revenge for past misdeeds? It wouldn't be the first case in history where someone has bided their time to get even. With one person, it's understandable someone might want to seek revenge against another person, but against three and maybe more?"

"More? Goodness me, really, Inspector?" Joan Rigby leaned forward.

April quickly realised that she might have revealed too much and swiftly changed tack. "When he spoke with a colleague, your son mentioned that Stanley Cooper used to visit your home. Is that so? When was that?"

"Stan?" She chuckled briefly. "Dear Stan. Goodness he had a wicked sense of humour, all innuendo and double entendre. He'd done well and held a senior position in the LEA. John and he were good friends, as were Seex and Colin Drummond although I can't remember either of them coming to the house. I know the name Seex made Ian laugh and blush. He wasn't that old at the time. I know that they all had a bit of a reputation. Being in the profession one hears rumours but I believed there was no real substance to them or so I thought. I only discovered the truth just before we separated. I should have remembered the old adage about smoke and fire! It was funny what came out after that and I discovered other gentlemen were playing games too. It was all quickly swept under the carpet. A gentleman's club with few gentlemen, you know what I'm saying?"

April gave a gentle nod in agreement.

"People who were so-called friends had kept things hidden from me. I suppose that was to spare my feelings and not wanting to be the one to cause a potential break up. Years later, those three were part of a Facebook friends' group, Pedagogues' Place. Ian told me that he'd helped his dad get involved, guided him through the technology. I know when John had to retire, he missed the camaraderie, if I can put it that way, seems more delicate."

"And you?"

"I carried on teaching. People knew, of course. Real friends rallied round me especially when I bought this place. Ian came with me and after a while when I knew that I could pay the bills, I went part time to ensure my son got the best possible new start. I wanted to be home for him. I'm proud to say that he's done well for himself. Don't ask if I'm pleased that he followed me into the teaching profession." She shrugged her shoulders. "That's about it."

"Pedagogues' Place. Did you join?"

Joan did not answer immediately. "After what I'd been through. No!"

Chapter Eighteen

Cyril had vowed never to accept the old maroon Bentley after his father had left it to him in his will. It held too many painful memories. The pressure, however, brought to bear by Wendy, his stepmother, and Julie had made him see things from a different perspective. Fred too, Julie's father, had offered to cherish and look after the car so that he could drive it on the occasions he wanted. Against his better judgement the arrangement suited him.

Fred had the car waiting outside his garage. The engine sitting at tick over was barely audible. The only telltale sign the engine was running was a small curl of white-grey smoke appearing from the exhaust.

The car that dropped Cyril at the front of the house pulled away. It was then he saw the Bentley. The lustre polished into the chrome and paintwork glinted in the late afternoon sunshine. He approached Fred who was just wiping the windscreen with some kitchen roll. Cyril patted his shoulder.

"Looks magnificent, Fred. Goodness you've used a few gallons of elbow grease on that!"

Fred laughed. "And the rest but the old girl's well worth it. It gives me an excuse to escape into the garage and I don't have to sit in front of the box and watch soaps."

"I'm grateful and so is she." Cyril patted the car's huge radiator.

"Fettling this old girl is better than sitting in front of the idiot's lantern any day of the week!"

Cyril had always used the term for the television and Fred had soon adopted it.

"Started first time, Cyril. I've checked everything. There's even a full tank of fuel. I'll pass the bill on later. I take it Julie's unaware of this evening's plan?"

Cyril nodded. "It'll be some time on our own but I'm sure work will come into the conversation." He winked. "Better move. Thank you very much. I'll bring it back tomorrow evening after work if that's okay?"

"Drive carefully and give my daughter a kiss from me."

Fred popped up his thumb and stood back watching the driver's door close. It always seemed incongruous the door should open opposite to that of a modern car. 'Suicide doors' was not a name to dwell on. The engine note lifted slightly as the Bentley whispered out through the gate towards the town and within ten minutes, Cyril would be at Robert Street.

***

Sonia Dawson had come home earlier than normal. She had felt a sixth sense that something was wrong. It grew stronger and more uncomfortable as she approached the house. A tingle ran across her shoulders and up the nape of her neck. Looking up at the bedroom window brought further concern. It was there and clear to see, something was different. The front bedroom curtains, those in Martin's room were not how she had left them before going to work. Controlling her shaking hand, she slipped the key into the lock whilst cautiously pushing open the door. She saw the shoes, Martin's shoes and the coat she did not recognise then she saw the note attached to the fridge. A wave of relief flooded her body and her legs felt weak as she crossed the kitchen. She stared at the note:

I'm sorry Mum x.

Lifting the magnet, she took the sheet. Tears came to her eyes and she slumped onto a stool bringing the now scrunched-up paper to her chest. It was as if a huge weight had been lifted from her shoulders. Regaining her composure, she went upstairs. The door to Martin's room was slightly ajar. There was nothing from the television and no music. She tapped on the door before opening it fully. Martin was on the bed wrapped in his dressing gown, a pile of clothes was dumped on the floor. Turning to look at her his face said everything. It was a mixture of fear and sadness. Swinging his legs off the bed he moved quickly towards her and wrapped her within his arms. Waiting for him to speak she just hugged him, eyes closed, her nose drawing in the familiar smell of his hair. He said nothing.

"Have you eaten today?"

Martin shook his head. "Sorry!" He began to sob.

She held him closer. "We can sort this. We can sort it. No matter what's happened I will always love you. You will, Martin, always be my best boy."

An hour later, David Owen and Donna James, the police Family Liaison Officer, sat opposite Martin and Sonia Dawson. Her other two children had been collected from school and were with her parents. On the small table between them was the envelope and what remained of the hundred pounds. Owen carefully collected it and slipped it into a plastic Forensic bag before adding a note to the affixed label. He doubted there would be any fingerprints remaining or critical Forensic evidence but it was standard procedure. Martin had gone through the whole story. He offered names where he knew them. Owen moved outside briefly and made a call. There was a need to liaise with officers in Leeds and arrange for the house in Harehills to be watched and then checked.

"Will-o'-the-wisps, Martin, that's what these people are. They lure youngsters away with their shiny gifts and false promises. You're dispensable and disposable. What they want is to get you to enjoy the drugs too and once you become addicted they have you. That would become their method of paying you. I know it was traumatic, the motorbike, but it's as if your father protected you. Brought you home safely. They'll have others just like you. They don't care about you as a person, they only care about what you can do for them. It's only business to them. You will know very little about them, they made sure of that. The house, it will be empty or will have a cover story. They, Star and those you saw in the house and car, will have just moved to another place. It's like chess to them, it's a game, but a game that costs young lives."

Owen paused and looked at the lad opposite. He felt a pang of sadness. This was happening more and more around the country as the gangs spread their cancerous tentacles more widely.

Martin delved into his jumper and withdrew a plastic bag. "It's a bandana. It belongs to Star. She wore it yesterday and I took it. It smells of her." A tear came to his eyes and ran down his cheek before he wiped it with the back of his hand. "I don't know why but I put it in here, maybe to protect the smell and keep it safe for longer."

Owen looked at his colleague and then back to Martin before taking the bag. "Did she give you this?"

Martin shook his head. "I stole it. I'm sorry."

Before he left, Owen explained to them both he had not done wrong and things would work out. Donna was to finalise the arrangements for the next day's meeting. They were reassured that immediate security procedures would be put in place and arrangements made for them to be collected and brought to the police station the following morning. Owen needed to arrange a fast courier to take the items to the Forensics lab.

***

As they passed through Ripon, the smile on Julie's face said everything. The warmth of the car seemed to extract a combined aroma of old leather and warm oil from the old interior. It was comforting. The front bench seat allowed her to sit more closely to Cyril. "So, Cyril Bennett, it's not an Appleton's pork pie and a beer sitting on a public bench by the obelisk, I hope."

Cyril said nothing as he turned towards West Tanfield. "I had my fingers crossed the weather would improve. It's so beautiful around here." Within half an hour the Bentley crossed the bridge over the River Ure and on entering Masham, immediately turned right.

"The White Bear how lovely!" Julie clapped her hands quietly. "I know just what I'll be ordering." She leaned sideways and kissed his cheek.

The promise of not talking about work was often only broken after the main course was finished and it was so on this occasion as they settled to enjoy the cheese and biscuits. As he ordered a port, Julie grew more concerned over the quantity of alcohol he had consumed throughout the meal.

"You've had a lot to drink, is that wise?"

Cyril slipped his hand into his pocket and withdrew a key attached to a large fob. "It will mean an early breakfast and start but I booked a room too."

Julie slipped her hand on his. "What a clever man you are. Perfect."

"They've found the missing kid, the one linked to the drug packages. Came home on his own. Owen called when I was putting the case in the room. I packed some bits and bobs for you. Caner called too this afternoon talking about concentrated poisons and crystallisation. He has more for me. Two other potential poison victims have been named but they're still alive and kicking. Hopefully when we collate what we find from them, what we know and what we're discovering all the time, we'll be a step closer. The funnel will get ever narrower and the focus keener, which will take our investigation further."

"Anything linking from the dead men's IT or phones?"

"All part of that same Facebook group but no real personal communication between them. It would appear that over the years they've grown apart. From all accounts, they seemed fine at these meetings. Got on well, clearly old buddies with a lot of laughter from their chosen corner. For me, everything points to someone who was there, someone present at each meeting and able to add something into the food or drinks."

"Better than that, Cyril, specific people's food." She picked up a grape from the cheese board and leaned towards Cyril. He instinctively opened his mouth. "Accepted willingly food from someone they trust, maybe."

Cyril's jaw stopped moving momentarily and then he began to eat the offering. "You are clever. Cooper's wife was at one of the meets even though she didn't mention it at interview and we have a witness who saw her collect and deliver food from the buffet for him."

"It could be as easy as I've just demonstrated to you – it's all about trust."

"The crystals, the strong poison. Would they not be crunchy? Surely you'd know you'd taken them." Cyril picked up more cheese.

"They would be ground into a fine powder and then added to food or drink. Of course, you would need to keep the dose concentrated and not drown it in a pint. Added to port would be just perfect. Dark colour, strong flavour." She slid her finger across her throat.

Cyril looked at the port in front of him. "Right. I see."

Chapter Nineteen

April could not sleep. She stood in the kitchen leaning against the sink and staring out at the breaking day. The jagged, orange-red line that ran across the low, eastern sky looked like a sore and inflamed scar. Ralph, her Great Dane, was curled up on the sofa oblivious to the early morning movement until he heard the rattle of his lead. Her mind had been full, ideas from snippets of conversation and interviews contrived to deny her any peaceful rest. Admitting defeat, she decided to walk the dog and then get into work early. There was something nagging her and she knew the answer was there on the boards in the Incident Room, hiding in plain sight. It would just be a case of finding it.

She had adopted Ralph after his owner had been savagely killed. On that occasion they had been just too late to save her. The police were there but owing to the circumstances, they could do nothing to stop the woman's death. No family members wanted the dog. Either Ralph would be destroyed, go into kennels or home with her. It had been one of the best decisions she had ever made. Scratching his ear, she bent and kissed the top of his head. "Let's hope we don't make the same mistake again with this one, Ralph, we've lost enough already."

Ralph yawned as a back leg came up to scratch the side of his neck.

The Stray was quiet. Large and in some cases deep puddles had formed in the hollows within the grass, black mirrors of reflected light set against the grey ground. Unlike many dogs, Ralph avoided water at all costs as if his paws were so delicate, they would dissolve on contact. His paw placement was precise until he started to run and then the gangling creature morphed into an athlete. He became fluid, like moving water itself. Every muscle and sinew worked in harmony as he built up speed. It was pure grace. April ran and he followed, swiftly passing her and then doubling back. It never ceased to amaze her just how fast he could move but also how quickly he would tire. He was clearly built for sprints and not for marathons. Within minutes of returning home, he had taken a drink, found his favourite spot, lowered his undercarriage and folded his body ready for more sleep.

"I do envy you some days, Ralph Richmond."

Just at that moment, the dog answered with a snore as if to rub salt into her wound.

***

It was an hour later when Cyril stood in the car park of The White Bear. He too was delighted that the day dawned bright with a clear sky. Cyril had already packed the car and finished breakfast. He planned to drop Julie off at home and then go straight to the police station. He knew he would get some derogatory comments about a Chief Inspector's pay as he pulled up to put the Bentley into the secure car park. He always did. What with that and the number of people who referred to him as Morse. If they had read the books, they would know it was a Lancia he drove. It was a Jaguar in the television series. It was never a Bentley. Maybe it was the colour that confused them.

***

The porridge tasted particularly bitter and thicker in consistency than usual but it would still be eaten, only maybe not as quickly. The jigsaw was growing daily, looking more like the original photograph. The unusual, modern design of the building stood out starkly against the blue sky. The ground and most of the shrubs that bordered the group of people were also completed. The reds of the roses and the simple yet spectacular yellow of the daisies to either side of the group of people, brought back memories of happier times. The lower portions of many of the group had also been found and finished; they were now a decapitated collective as they stood facing the camera. The porridge finished, one more piece hovered over the jigsaw before the correct place was located and another moment of satisfaction was achieved.

***

Owen was waiting and Cyril was disappointed that he failed to comment on his morning's mode of transport.

"Not walked, sir? Unusual that!" Turning, he scratched his head and escorted Cyril towards his office. "Martin and his mum are in today and I'm hoping for some Forensic results on one or more of the gang members. I've tagged them as a priority. Martin's agreed to look through some mugshots of known and suspected dealers and then have a go with photofit. I plan to get something out on the website, I want them to know he's with us. Our colleagues in Leeds have checked the house where Martin says he stayed for two nights but it's empty, cleaned but traces of his DNA were found. He's telling the truth, a supposed break-in the

159

landlord is protesting. I checked the area and it's one of those neighbourhoods where you see all, hear all and say nowt. Even the front doors have bloody bars. You get the distinct impression that everyone is looking after themselves. The barriers are strong and high for a reason."

"You may well be right. I need ten minutes of your precious time, Owen. Are you sure you want to release the information so quickly?" Cyril ushered him down the corridor. "You've done the Health and Safety assessments, considered the family's personal security needs, I take it?"

Owen shook his head. "Thought it was import …" He did not finish.

"Take the appropriate steps, cover every base precisely and follow the correct procedures. I've told you before, Owen, it should always be like this with planning. You imagine that you're throwing a pebble into a still, deep pond. Do you turn and walk away as soon as you've chucked it in?"

"No, sir, you wait and watch. You look where all of the ripples end up as they are the result of your initial throw. Only when the pond returns to calm do you move on after noting every effect of your action."

"Good, Owen, good. And that's key in this case where minors are concerned. If anything were to happen after our involvement, your organisation, Inspector …" Cyril emphasised Owen's new title. "It will be on your head, and more importantly mine, that the weight from above will fall. I want those assessments on my desk before anything is released to the public. Imagine the lad to be your son and act accordingly. Now for those ten minutes I requested. What time is Martin due?"

"Ten o'clock, sir."

"You have enough time. Come. Chuck that brick in the pond, Owen, and then watch."

Owen reluctantly made a call.

Cyril pushed open the door and they walked through into the Incident Room used in relation to the poisonings.

April had been in the station since six-thirty along with Shakti and three other officers. On a freestanding whiteboard near a desk were written two names, those of Ingrid Cooper and Caroline Peet. Beneath were added the key elements for the investigation Cyril had requested. Chemistry knowledge, foot size and garden lovers. There were also bullet points – motive, ability to commit the acts, reason – then the word *Cluedo* was followed by the words: *Who, with what and why*?

April stood when she saw Cyril approaching. "Thanks for coming early, sir. I'd like to request we get these two people in for further in-depth questioning. Interestingly, Ingrid Cooper called to give two names she has remembered, Drummond and Foster, who had links to her husband. I've added them to the board. We know of them both. I'd like a warrant to search their properties." She picked up a black felt pen and added 'UR/WYS' followed by '88' and '91'. "Yesterday I spoke with John Rigby's ex-wife. It was something she'd said during our chat that's troubled me. It was in reference to the harm parents do psychologically to their offspring, particularly if they overcompensate for their actions. I made a note but it didn't hit me straight away. It came back to me later when I was at home and it worried me all night. When I was running with Ralph this morning it literally dawned on me and hence, I was in here earlier than I should have been." She wrote – *You Reap / What You Sow.* She tapped on the words. "They're not initials at all like we first believed. It's a specific pointer to an act and a date, maybe a betrayal or a misdeed."

There was a moment's silence as both Cyril and Owen contemplated what had just been said. It was certainly plausible.

Owen was the first to break the silence. "Martin's mother said that too but not those exact words. She mentioned how parenting was so hard and in some circumstances she'd had to be cruel to be kind, but that action in itself caused problems and a dilemma for her. It's the same with April's example, but the reverse – being too kind could be equally cruel – spoiled child syndrome! She didn't have a partner to back her up or even to discuss whether she was doing the right thing." Concern for her was clearly etched on Owen's face as he spoke. "I guess I was lucky during my growing up. We didn't have the same materialistic, social pressures. You only see how lucky you were later in life."

"Or not, as the case may be. Single parenting is not easy, I guess," Shakti added.

"How old would Rigby and Cooper have been then in 88 and 91?" Cyril asked whilst looking for the birth dates of both victims.

"Rigby would have been 36 in '88 and Cooper 38 in '91. Both were married according to this and both worked within this LEA."

Cyril rested his backside on the edge of one of the desks. "The people linked so far in this investigation are all within his peer group, all about the same age. Surely if their philandering has anything to do with their deaths, their reaping would have been challenged. It's more than likely to be consensual between adults."

"You've heard of the *Me Too* movement, sir?" Shakti added. "Remember there were no reports of any of the women present at either meeting feeling ill. That puzzled me."

"I understand and see your point Shakti, and yours too April, they are both valid. So, what about Seex?" Cyril looked directly back at April. "Have we found those markings in relation to his death?"

"In some ways he's the anomaly as he's still married and there's no hidden message. His death was no different from that of Cooper, clearly it had the appearance of being accidental and possibly borne of his medical condition. We may have just not looked in the relevant place. Remember, those details were written within the grime on the back of Cooper's car. Had we not picked up on the one written on the bench, then that found on his car might well have been missed. Seex, being the first death, initially nobody considered it to be anything other than a cruel accident. We didn't know for what or where we were looking. Interestingly, the only letters and date that could have been written after the event was for Rigby but then we found others along the route he would have taken daily so it can be safely assumed that they too were posted pre rather than post death."

"We'll still have the car in the secure compound, I take it?" Cyril asked an obvious question.

April nodded before she turned and directed Nixon to

organise a further check, giving specific guidance to Forensics. Looking back at Owen and Cyril she added, "His wife is still in the family home. It was checked as soon as his death was put in Category Two with further assessment when it went to Category One. Mrs Seex has been fully co-operative. She has no recollection of seeing any markings. Strangely, she's holding up well. A strong woman." She paused and tapped the computer screen. "The results are on file. There was nothing discovered of any significance." She tapped it again. "The Forensic photographs are on file. I'll organise a closer inspection, but I feel we're wasting valuable resources and as SIO I'd rather look into Rigby and Peet."

Owen shuffled, eager to leave, believing his ten minutes were up. He made a deliberate show by checking his watch. Cyril glared at him. "You have time, Owen."

He shuffled further before trying to make amends. "I looked through the notes on here when I had a spare minute." He moved to a specific portion of the whiteboard whilst emphasising the words, *spare minute*. "This might be a stupid question, but have we checked the CCTV from the last venue, you know, where they met that had the possible food poisoning incident? The Wayfarers I believe?"

April was swift to respond. "They only maintain their digital recordings for the stipulated time as the system is on a loop. Four weeks. We were out by one week."

"What about photographs taken by those present? You have a list of those who attended. Did any take group pictures or selfies and the like?"

April raised her eyebrows. She was obviously impressed by Owen. "No, and I'm sure it's worth a request.

We do have the addresses and contact details of those present."

"One other thing before I go." He turned to look at Cyril. "I'd try for CCTV from the first venue. I believe Burton, I think it was." He ran his finger close to the board and flicked up a few sheets of paper attached to clips. "Yes, here, a Mrs Barbara Burton. She states they moved to The Wayfarers because of a similar problem with the previous venue. It's a long shot but for the sake of a phone call ... Do you have a date for that meeting?"

Cyril put a hand on Owen's shoulder. "Keen as mustard as usual, Owen."

He took that as his cue to leave.

As Cyril followed, April directed Shakti to seek photographs that might have been taken at The Wayfarers or the first venue by those in attendance. "Start with Barbara Burton and ask her to make the request. It may be less intimidating and quicker in the long run."

April looked again at the evidence. After more thought she decided to interview Caroline Peet and Joan Rigby in their homes. The warrant could wait until more evidence was garnered.

Chapter Twenty

Caroline Peet waited as the officers laid out various pieces of equipment and notepads. She displayed more confidence than many would in her position when confronted by the request for a further interview and questioned in her own home by two detectives. Her manner did not alter as April cautioned her. April had expected to see some changes within her demeanour but saw only a flush appear across her cheeks and a look of confusion, that was all. She seemed neither fazed nor unduly concerned.

In preparation, April had read the notes made during her previous visit. She had described Peet's positive and relaxed outlook on life and that even the tribulations of her past and the death of one, or maybe more, old lovers seemed to cause little distress. She had wondered whether that was through Peet living on her own for so long and never marrying and the selfishness that might bring. She quickly tried to brush over that knowing that she, if she were not careful, was heading in the same direction.

"Thank you for seeing me again, this is DC Nixon. He will be recording our interview but we felt it was better to talk here rather than at the station. When I spoke on the phone you told us you wore a size seven shoe."

Caroline Peet frowned initially and then nodded. "I do. Size twelve clothes although I feel more comfortable with a fourteen top." Her answer was in monotone as if being pointedly sarcastic. She paused. "I'm sorry, that sounds flippant but what's this to do with Stan? I'm assuming that this is still to do with Stan?"

"Do you own a pair of Skechers, Ms Peet?"

"Two pairs." She stood and left the room returning with two boxes. Lifting the lids of both she extracted a shoe from each. "I've worn this pair more."

The shoes were immaculate. A shoe tree protruded from each.

"If you think I've more and I'm keeping them hidden from you then you're welcome to search. I've nothing to hide. I didn't kill any of the men who have died recently. I wouldn't waste my time and I certainly wouldn't risk my autumnal years being locked up in some shitty little cell for any of them. I take it you've found evidence and that includes a shoe print of a Sketcher sole at a crime scene. Let me guess. Size? It's a size seven?"

April picked up the shoes and compared both against the image she had received from the Forensics database. Neither was an exact match.

"You look disappointed, Inspector Richmond. Please search the house, the garden the greenhouse. If you pardon the pun, fill your boots! This is silly. I need a coffee. Anyone else?"

"Before you do, and may I remind you that you're still under caution, did the Coopers know of your father's profession?"

Peet looked puzzled. "Father's profession? What's that got to do with anything?"

"Did they know?"

She shrugged her shoulders, the action itself answering the question before she spoke. "Maybe, many of my friends and colleagues knew. When he was here, living with me, he would help them with their gardens, not the Coopers of course, but then she'd buggered off quite soon after our dalliance. Strangely, Pops was here with me when she called one day as bold as brass and gave me the rounds of the kitchen, screaming such lovely terms as *sexual predator* and *whore*. I remember he just sat there where you're sitting now with his unlit pipe. He winked at me every now and then as she ranted on. He was such a love. I do miss him."

"How did he help your friends?" Nixon asked.

"I think that being involved with nature, with gardens, is what gave him life, kept him moving and active. He helped in their gardens and looked on the requests as a challenge. He didn't do the heavy digging or lifting, he just advised. He loved the gardening programmes on television and the radio but would often argue with the box telling them they were full of … manure might be the correct term. He was a Yorkshireman and a down-to-earth one at that!"

April looked across at Nixon. "Off the record, we'll both have a coffee if you're still in the mood to make one."

Caroline Peet suddenly relaxed as she looked at each officer and wondered what the bloody hell they were playing at. She stood and went to the kitchen.

On returning, Nixon restarted the recording.

"I managed to take him to the Southport Garden Festival on a couple of occasions. I don't think he was overly impressed."

"Did your father help John Rigby's wife?" She glanced

at her notes. "Joan?"

"He did. She was a lovely lady and no, I didn't have a relationship with Dr John although he would have been more than willing to have a dalliance. As I was peripatetic, I was one who really didn't need the promotion these men often purported to be able to influence. I had all the work I needed and I could also teach from home privately if I needed extra cash. She moved when they split and found a lovely end cottage in Killinghall. He usually drove but there was the odd occasion when I dropped him off there when he was helping to design the garden. If my memory serves me well, the garden wasn't huge but it ran along the back and the side. He designed the entrance gate, a kind of stone archway. Pretty it was too."

"Did he visit often?" April was much more relaxed and convinced Caroline had nothing to do with any of the murders.

"He did the drawings and added the names of the shrubs and the planting and seating areas. He also made space to accommodate a greenhouse even though she couldn't afford to build it at the time. If I'm honest, I think he helped her out there as he had contacts and could get things like that at a considerable discount. When he returned, he would often talk about her lad, Callum, or was it Ian? His name escapes me. How he would roll his sleeves up and get stuck in. He took a shine to him. Said he'd make a good gardener's apprentice."

**

Owen was waiting at the same spot in which he had been that morning when Cyril arrived. He watched the police car draw through the security gates and enter the garage area.

It would be a few minutes before Sonia and Martin Dawson appeared. After his pointed conversation with Cyril, Owen had arranged for a manager within the Youth Justice Service to be present to start a support programme for Martin and the family. He needed to dot every I and cross every T with this case. Liaising with the YJS ensured a life coach and a clinical psychologist would be available to support the boy and his family.

On arrival, Martin looked decidedly scared but on seeing Owen, a shallow smile came to his lips. He had decided he liked the big gentle man. His mother's protective arm helped lead him towards Owen who put out his hand. Martin felt the same uncertainty he had experienced in Leeds when the stranger proffered the same gesture. This time, however, he shook it with a degree of firmness. He wanted it to mean something, he wanted to be friends.

***

"Ms Peet, you mentioned when I was last here that your father kept diaries and records and you had them in the loft."

"That's right. I haven't had time to go through them but I promised myself that one day I would. Why?"

"Did your father continue his journals, diaries and things when he was here living with you and working on your friends and neighbours' gardens?"

"I think so. Everything went into a box when he died. To be honest with you, I was in two minds whether to chuck them out as they'd be painful to look through, especially the photographs he took."

Nixon looked across at April. "May we look through them either here or at the station?"

***

Martin sat with his mother looking at the large wall screen as a number of faces momentarily stared back. He was confident using the remote to forward, pause or reverse them. A can of coke sat on the table in front of him and his mother nursed her second coffee of the day. As an image flipped onto the screen Martin dropped the remote. Staring back was the face he had seen in the house, the Asian man whose mouth said one thing but his eyes another. Owen noted the number to the lower right of the photograph.

"Who's that, Martin?" Owen bent to retrieve the remote and the psychologist, observing from another room, leaned forward to monitor Martin's reactions.

"I don't know who he is and I only saw him once. They called him Tea as in the brew and not the letter. He gave me the money and told me I was doing well. He promised me things, trainers … He scared me. He pretended to like me but I knew it wasn't genuine."

"You're safe. Well done! That's a great help. Do you want to carry on?"

Leaning for the remote he nodded and started the slides moving. It would be a further ten minutes before he paused it again.

"Star!" he whispered as the young girl's face filled the screen. His lip quivered. "I trusted her and I liked her. She knew about Dad. She knew how I felt about bikes." He turned to look directly at Owen. "How could she do that to me? She said she loved me. How could she send someone to pick me up on a motorbike, how?"

Owen felt an immediate lump hit the back of his throat and a tick appeared in his eye, as if a speck had settled there blown by a non-existent wind. An anger quickly brewed within him. Managing to keep control, he stood and briefly left the room. Sonia immediately hugged her son.

"The bitch. How could she string an adolescent lad, an innocent who'd been through enough, on like that? What promises did she make?" Owen's words went unheard but he immediately saw the connection with Cooper and his colleagues – the vultures – bastards each and every one.

After regaining his composure, Owen returned. He walked directly over to Martin and put a hand on his shoulder. "You're a brave lad and your family loves you. Not everyone could do what you've done over these last few hours. You should be proud. Remember this, my young friend, we'll all make mistakes in our lives, mistakes that will not only affect us but those whom we truly love. It's not about the mistakes, Martin, it's about how we sort them, how we put them right. That's what takes the courage. On the way we'll be tempted and tricked by people who'll promise this and threaten that. They may profess to look after you and tell you that they love you. They're not what or who they say they are and sometimes we only find that out when it's too late. I'm proud of you, Martin, and I know your mum and Nan and Grandad are too. You know what? I bet your dad would be as well."

Martin's lip quivered some more before the floodgates opened. He leaned forward and grabbed Owen.

"Sorry, Dad! Sorry!"

Owen looked at Sonia and mouthed, "It's okay."

***

Once at the top of the loft ladder, Nixon was directed by an impatient Peet. He had attached a head torch to his forehead but the light barely penetrated the darkness.

"Don't you go shoving your size nines through my lounge ceiling, Mr, or there will be hell to pay! Keep on the boards. They should be behind the box that's marked, 'Christmas Tree'."

She looked at April and frowned. "Men! If you want anything doing ..."

Chapter Twenty-One

Shakti threw a fist into the air when the venue that hosted the previous reunion confirmed that they still had the CCTV footage for that day. It would be forwarded once the paperwork was in place to release the data. With that, and the possibility of photographs coming in from those present, it meant they should have a better understanding of who was where, when and importantly who met with whom.

**

The morning was fine and the forecast was good for the whole day but Melanie Masters had tucked a small umbrella into her bag. The weather seemed so capricious of late and she had only been to the hairdresser's the day before. The weather reports on the radio seemed more a lottery than an accurate interpretation of meteorological facts. The weather station she had set up in her last school had a greater prediction success rate. She trusted no one.

Passing the Cenotaph, she paused for a moment, something she had always done. It took a second or two from her day to honour those who had sacrificed a lifetime. Her mother had always stopped and she saw no reason not to maintain this respectful tradition.

As always, the traffic flow down Parliament Street was constant even though it was a one-way road. She pressed her finger on the button on the Pelican Crossing and waited. It seemed to take an age until the shrill signal announced she and the other pedestrians could then cross. She should have walked down Montpellier Hill but she veered slightly off track to admire the display of cakes in Betty's Tearoom window. The Fat Rascals always appealed but not today, she would forgo the pleasure. The shop, as usual, was busy and a small queue had already formed for the café.

Her day was mapped out. She had planned to drop a bag of items into her favourite charity shop and then go on to have lunch. In all the time she had been supporting the shop it had always had a peculiar smell. It was an aroma that was difficult to describe, it being neither truly pungent nor pleasant. On some occasions it was worse than others. Today was one of those days. Nobody who worked there knew from whence it came and they tended to over compensate with aerosols and joss sticks. The landlord had investigated, looking in the obvious places, the drains and the electrical wiring. He had found nothing. Melanie remembered a story she had heard where a thief had tried to break into a jeweller's shop via the chimney. He had been successful until renegotiating the climb back up with bulging pockets. He became wedged. Nobody knew he was there and that is where he stayed until his skeleton was discovered over fifty years later during renovation work. She chuckled as she told the assistant the story and they both looked at the bricked up fireplace.

"You just never know as fact can often be stranger than fiction. I'm sure it's apocryphal. Would produce a smell though! What was this shop in the fifties?" Melanie asked as she turned to leave, not waiting for the answer and pulling the door open, awakening the bell once again. Back outside, the fresh air was a marked change and she stood and enjoyed a few deep breaths.

Since the deaths of three of the group, the difficulties faced with the venues, and some of the group's future, more formal meetings had been put on hold. Members, however, had decided to form their own splinter groups. This had always happened at the meetings where those who worked within the same school tended to congregate and it seemed natural that they should do so now. Not all those using Pedagogues' Place had the same interests or reasons for attending.

Melanie was early and found an empty bench facing the sun. The traffic was light. She watched as a solitary man, positioned on the far pavement, was being interviewed to camera and wondered what he was doing and more importantly, who he might be. She removed her phone and surreptitiously took a photograph so she could study it later. If she did not know who he was, the others she was meeting for lunch might.

Colin Drummond was the first to arrive. He had missed the last meeting and had been saddened to hear of the deaths of members of the group. He was alone. His wife was unable to attend but she had encouraged him to go. Moving towards the bar he ordered a white wine. He had decided to find a table outside positioned near the lawn. It gave a clear view down Swan Lane and the Mercer Art Gallery. Two people sat at one table and a single woman at another. She had a tray of coffee and was reading a paper. He counted the chairs – he believed he would need seven if he remembered correctly. Checking his watch, he was fifteen minutes early. Leaving his glass and his coat to secure the table, he turned to the lady.

"Excuse me for disturbing you. I need to get more chairs. Could you just ensure nobody sits here? I'll only be a moment or two."

She smiled and nodded. "Certainly."

He went inside to request more chairs and within minutes he returned, followed by a member of the hotel staff carrying three more. Turning to thank the lady she was just about to leave.

"I've left you my newspaper. I've read it and unfortunately done the crossword. Not much in it, only depressing news these days. I hope you and your friends," she looked at the growing ring of chairs, "have a lovely lunch. It was no problem."

"Thank you. Thank you very much. We'll try!"

Drummond watched her walk down the drive. His eyes scanned her figure before stopping at her ankles, he had always had a thing about ankles. Collecting his glass, he raised it. "To shapely ankles. I'll always drink to that. Cheerio!" Lifting the glass, he sipped the wine before returning to the table. Picking up the newspaper she had kindly left, he settled down to await the others.

***

Owen had assured Martin that his family would be looked after and secure but, should they find the two people he had identified, then he would be asked to give evidence using a video link. Initially reluctant, Martin had agreed he could do it.

Even though it was Owen's two-day break, he contacted the lead agency responsible for ensuring the Dawsons' welfare. The family move to her parents' house for the foreseeable future was encouraged and considered to be a sensible move. That and the installation of temporary, centrally monitored house and personal alarms, gave peace of mind to all parties.

The DNA link from the bandana and the identified photograph matched that of Fiona Hunt aged eighteen. According to the police central database records she had one previous conviction for drug dealing. A general wanted notice for her had been quickly secured along with that of the identified Asian. It was, after looking at the evidence, unlikely that they would target Martin. He was a small fish and it had been suggested by the Drugs' Investigation Team that Martin had been set up and had failed a test. He was therefore now superfluous, unlike Hunt who had found his weakness. She would be moved to a different location in the UK. For a pretty, young girl, picking damaged and lonely lads off the street was the easy part and retribution would be the last thing on their minds. Getting kids to follow instructions to the letter was more challenging. If past experiences were to count, those operating the line would want the ripples to settle as quickly as possible and no further action would be taken. There was, however, always that chance and as Cyril had said, every precaution necessary should be taken.

***

The two boxes were poignantly marked with the title, *Dad's Life's Work.* They sat empty at one end of the table and the contents had been spread down either side. Caroline Peet had agreed to release them on the understanding they would be returned as found. She was still unsure why her father's jottings, drawings and photographs were relevant to the police in such a serious case, but she had her suspicions after the interview and on hearing the rumours circulating on the net that all three had been poisoned. Inspector Richmond and DC Nixon had been very tight-lipped. Her father had died a few years before all of this so she had little to worry about.

The journals detailing the early years were of little use to April. Cyril handled the books and files with care as he sat reading the entries for the year 1953.

"He was certainly a skilled horticulturist looking at the results of his work for the Coronation displays set out around the city of Bradford. It's just a pity many of the photographs are in black and white. The news cuttings from the *Bradford Telegraph and Argus* are praise indeed." Cyril tapped the page. "Impressive!"

April wanted him to concentrate on the later years but he assured her that by working through them chronologically he would know the man and that, in turn, might help when interpreting the later diaries. Besides, it was not every day you could see diaries demonstrating the life of an everyday working man. The skills of most of these stalwarts of society had long been lost and forgotten.

"According to his marriage certificate, John Rigby was married in 1972." She paused. "Goodness, the same year their son, Ian was born ..."

Cyril looked up. "Nothing unusual there then, April. Rushed marriage, I guess. Marry in haste and then repent at leisure or split up. When did they separate?"

"Ian was nine or ten. That would make it 1982 and she bought the house in Killinghall in late '82. According to Peet, her father moved to Harrogate to live with her in 1991.

Born in 1921 that made him seventy. He died in 2001 and so he must have worked at Joan Rigby's and the other gardens locally any time after 1991. We know in Rigby's case she wouldn't have been able to afford to do much work in the early years and even when she did, Peet told me the greenhouse was planned for but added a little later."

April moved along the line in search of the correct dates. "Bingo!"

July 1993: Caroline asked if I could help an old colleague of hers plan a garden using many of the shrubs that she already has but also to add new hedging as planning had been granted to the open land at the back of the house and a small estate of houses was to be constructed. She was frightened of losing her privacy and hoped that I might be able to assist in selecting some fast-growing, evergreen coverage.

On arriving at the house, we talked about what she wanted and I drew up some plans. Included here.

April studied the drawings and identified the garden as that of Joan Rigby.

August 1993: Started the groundwork. It was good to have the young lad help along with Joan. There's nothing as keen as youth …"

April paused, took a piece of paper and subtracted 72 from 93. "Twenty-One!"

Turning to Cyril she posed the question. "Would someone refer to a man of twenty-one as a young lad?"

Cyril did not look up, keeping his head in the journal. "Depends on how old the person writing is."

"Seventy," April shot straight back.

"Possible. When I see some of our new coppers they

look like kids and that paramedic who was at the accident looked in her teens." He paused briefly before tapping the page he was looking at. "Look here, April, there are some handwritten herbal recipes, cures for headaches, stomach upsets. Goodness there's one for chilblains too. That takes me back. Not had those since I was a kid."

"There are also quite a few potions dotted through the other journals, including cures for animal illness too!"

***

Colin Drummond had finished his wine when he noticed both Norma and Melanie trundling past the Mercer Gallery with another lady in tow. From that distance he could not recognise her. Again, leaving his now empty glass, newspaper and coat, he went inside to the bar. Knowing those approaching, it would be two red wines and a white for himself. The mystery guest would have to wait. He collected the drinks on a tray and quickly turned, not seeing the gentleman who was heading for the same exit appear from behind. The glasses fell immediately and wine splashed Colin's shirt and jacket but he held on to the tray.

"I'm so sorry."

Colin turned to look at the person making the apology. Fortunately, he had survived with only a few spots of white wine on his jacket. He said nothing.

"It takes two to crash. Fifty-fifty according to insurance claims, I believe. You go and clean up and I'll replenish these and pop them on your table. Is it that one where the ladies are now sitting?"

Colin nodded. "Are you sure? That's kind. You're right, I should have looked."

"The least I can do."

The man carried a clean tray containing the drinks outside, pausing briefly at a table just inside the door. Watching the ladies settle he approached them.

"The gentleman you are expecting has had a small problem with a tumbling tray full of drinks and as I was partly to blame, I've refreshed them for you. Please accept these with my compliments. Three drinks but four people … Mum?" Ian looked at his mother sitting at the table. Trixie growled. He put the drinks down. "This white belongs to the gentleman. I'm missing one. Who can that be, mother?" He smiled at her.

"Norma and I are the red wine girls. Joan?"

"It will be a gin and tonic I believe, Mrs Rigby?" Ian held the tray as if he were a waiter.

Joan nodded. "What are you …"

"Educational conference, a day away from school. It's in the big room. I'll call in on my way home tonight, probably be about six. I'll get your drink." He turned and entered the room again placing his order. Colin paused as he passed the bar. "Your drinks are outside. Could you take this for the other lady? It's my mother! My apologies again. You've scrubbed up well!"

***

April picked up her phone and requested a call be made to Caroline Peet. Within minutes she was on the line. "Ms Peet, you had a very talented father. My boss has been admiring the work he did for the Coronation."

"I was barely a twinkle. You didn't ring to tell me that, Inspector."

"Some interesting recipes too."

"Concoctions, dear, get it right. As a kid I was brought

up on those. Hell, you dare not cough or complain in our house or some potion of his was thrust in some orifice."

April had to control her amusement. "You talked about Joan Rigby's garden and that her son helped your father. Do you know how old he was then?"

"My father or her son?"

"Sorry, yes, her son."

"No idea is the simple answer. I just recall that he took a shine to him. Surely with John Rigby's death you'll have all that information."

"In his notes your father refers to the young lad. Ian Rigby was twenty-one when your father worked there. Would he refer to someone that age as a young lad?"

Peet laughed. "He was lucky he used that term. Anyone younger, and I mean only by a few years, could be referred to as Sprog, Nipper or young Fellow-me-lad depending whether they were working under him. He had more respect for the general public so the use of the title lad was appropriate. Saying that, he even went through a phase where he called everyone Arthur as he could never remember names. He even addressed some woman by that name too! A real character I think the term is we use for people like my dad. It's been said of me too! Probably all the crap he used to dose me with. Mind, saying that, I've never had a day off work and I can cycle for miles." There was silence. "Is that it or can I confuse you some more, Inspector?" The giggle was infectious and April chuckled too.

"The more I get to know that woman, the more I like her." April returned to the journal.

"Then there's a clear case to keep an even more open

mind, April. Serial murderers become just that because people trust them. Just speaking from experience."

April knew Cyril had a point.

Chapter Twenty-Two

Owen sat with Hannah outside The New Inn at Appletreewick. The garden was set across and below the road from the pub, looking over the fields towards the River Wharfe. The day had seemed warm until they had stopped to sit and the breeze along the dale brought an edge, necessitating Owen bringing fleeces from the car.

"Black Sheep, Cyril's favourite ale of all time. He's a great boss, love, and so I raise my glass firstly to you, Hannah, the light of my life and then the man himself, Cyril Bennett. Cheers!"

She chuckled and drank a tomato juice. "Cyril ... and Julie. Not to forget my boss."

"Julie, yes. Appropriate that drink. Looks like blood in a cup! Surprised you've not tested it for the blood group."

"You say the sweetest ..." She did not finish before Owen chipped in.

"Did you know that when I was a kid I came here, not to the pub, but to Appletreewick with my school? Over yonder is Parcevall Hall and gardens. We went there to look at the gardens. It was owned by a really big bloke, six foot seven he was. He built the hall and had everything made for his height, the furniture and stuff but also the height of the sinks and toilet were amazing, so high." He demonstrated by raising his hands as if washing them in the tall bowl. "He was dedicated to the garden and plants, that was his life and so he was known as the *Gentle Giant*. I think he founded Harlow Carr Gardens in Harrogate but it's a long time since I was told that so I might be wrong. Anyway, they let us take a look inside and that's how I know about the size of things but it's closed to the public, only the gardens are open now."

"Suit you that!" Hannah mimicked his handwashing.

"When I win the lottery, maybe. Anyway, we went up Troller's Gill and we were told of a dog with saucer-sized eyes that attacked travellers. Christ, I couldn't sleep for a week when I got home and if I heard a dog bark I'd nip to my nan's room!"

"You love this place, North Yorkshire, don't you?"

"I loved Bradford but when my gran and grandad brought me out here it was like paradise. I'd play in the streams, make dams, walk, climb. I became so many people in my head when I played on my own. I'd be asleep by the time we reached home. Harrogate has been a wonderful place to work and live and now we have our home there we can get into the Dales at the drop of a hat."

She sipped her tomato juice taking care to wipe her mouth. "Do you have a favourite place in all the world, Owen?"

"I'd need a minute and another pint before I can answer that. My stomach thinks my throat's been cut too so I'll bring the menus." He stood, grinned and kissed the top of her head before crossing the road to the pub.

***

Two others quickly joined the group. Melanie spoke. "I hope that many of you will remember Joan. We were sorry to hear about John. It was luck just bumping into her this morning and I was so pleased you agreed to come for a chin wag and a bite to eat. Fancy that kind young lad being your son. What's the chance of that? Do you know everyone else?"

Drummond recognised Joan immediately. "I remember you vividly, you were such fun. We met on a few courses at the Teachers' Centre in Harrogate. Goodness, Joan, that's going back. You weren't called Rigby then. You were new into the teaching profession."

Joan smiled and nodded but did not answer the open question. She focused on Drummond as he waited, anticipating an answer but none came. He looked again at his stained jacket. She could not remember where she had met him before but she knew that she had and out of the blue the word *weasel* came to mind. It was his appearance.

Sipping her drink, she looked at Melanie. "We were together a long time ago, it's in the past, but thank you." Trixie jumped onto her lap. "What with the death of Paul Seex and Cooper. Do you all still get together and chat on Facebook? My son helped his dad with that. Never had a clue with technology, but neither do I. Just give me my jigsaws and my garden and I'm happy."

Barbara Burton walked quickly up the road like a ship in full sail. She carried a bag in either hand. Seeing the group already seated outside, she stopped, put both bags down, took a deep breath and waved as she stood at the hotel gates.

"Sorry, sorry boys and girls, the bus was late and I had two jobs to do. That post office gets busier. Can I get anyone a drink? Menus? Shall I get them?" Everyone was fine but they were happy to see what was available to eat.

She deposited her bags on the empty chair and went inside to get her drink.

"You live in Killinghall? Do you drive or get the bus?" Colin asked Joan as he lifted his drink. "Cheers."

"I drive in in the morning. I spoil myself by having a coffee in town near where I park, walk Trixie on The Stray and then it's home for the day. This morning I came in a little later than usual. I've not been as well as I'd like. Some days getting started is easier than others. If it wasn't for Trixie …"

***

Owen held Hannah's hand as he walked her through the formations that stood like sleeping giants to either side of the path for which Brimham Rocks was renowned.

"You asked where my favourite place was. I thought we should come and look. Many have names because of the way they look."

"They're stunning. I came here as a child too. I used to sit and look over the edge of a crag that was called Lover's Leap. The view was so special. I think it's over there."

Within ten minutes they were sitting on the edge. Huge boulders seemed to be jammed, locked together over the drop as if in an embrace.

"It's hardly changed. The trees are taller but the rest is the same. Some initials and dates are written into the stone. It always fascinated me how deeply some are carved."

Owen immediately thought of the markings found at the scenes of the two recent deaths.

"To think they will all be dead and yet they enjoyed just what we are doing now. Special places always trap special memories." She leaned over and kissed his cheek.

"Where's your very special place?"

Scrambling down and back onto the path Owen announced he'd be a moment. "Close your eyes and count slowly to thirty. She did and he disappeared.

"... twenty-seven, twenty-eight, twenty ..." She felt a tap on her shoulder. She looked at Owen. "Well?"

"I shouldn't have had three pints. I was desperate for a pee."

Hannah's swinging right hand caught his shoulder. "Men!"

"What? Come on. My favourite place is just up here."

Turning a bend and after a slight climb, Owen pointed to a huge boulder of rock balancing on the smallest of pedestals. "That's it. The Balancing Idol or the Druid's Idol. Someone thought it had been carved like that by the Druids. I used to dare myself to lie beneath it. Do you know, it was like a huge challenge as a kid? Imagine if I'd been here ..." he slid his arm next to the pedestal, "and this fell from above. That's two hundred tons balanced on that. It's no thicker than the top of my leg!"

"What's it made of?" Hannah pulled his arm out from beneath it. "Don't!"

"Rock!" Owen grinned, being deliberately obtuse. "It's millstone grit, Yorkshire grit. This was my favourite as a kid and it still is. It's like life when you think about it. It's in balance, steady, strong and you feel it will never tumble and then? You only need something to disturb it and your life, your world comes crashing down. Bit like that kid we're dealing with. A few months ago, he was in balance or people thought so, but the death of his dad had started the development of an invisible crack. There might be one, an invisible crack forming right in the middle of that bit of rock holding up this two-hundred-ton boulder, we just can't see it and neither do we expect it and then ... Fragile. Things are not always what we see on the surface."

"Too much Black Sheep, David Owen. Come on, let's get you home."

***

Barbara moved her bags after handing out the menus. "I've had a request from the police for any photographs taken at either of the last two meetings. I know we have some budding David Baileys in the group and so if you've taken and saved any selfies or group shots, I'd be grateful if you'd be kind enough to email them to me. I'll make sure the police get them. I'll add a reminder within Pedagogues' Post when I get home just in case. If you have a memory like mine, you'll need that jog!"

As Barbara took her seat, Colin Drummond stood shakily, putting a steadying hand on Barbara's shoulder. "Sorry, I must have drunk the first wine a little too enthusiastically, either that or my blood pressure has fallen. I need the loo, sorry. Please exc ..."

He did not finish. Turning, he swayed slightly but then found his equilibrium and entered the building.

Norma leaned forward mischievously. "As I've said in the past, some of the men have had a drink knocked over and so they swig it back just in case it happens again. He was bloody christened in the stuff today, Joan, by your son. Couldn't happen to a nicer chap."

"Enough, Norma. We're all friends here. Now what are we eating? I'll order and get Colin's when he returns." As she stood, Trixie jumped off Joan's lap. Its lead tangled with the table leg causing the table to shake. Joan stretched out to prevent her own glass from falling as did Barbara, only for Joan to knock Colin's glass onto the floor. It shattered.

"Mind the dog's paws, Joan," Melanie instructed, showing her concern.

"I'll get someone to come out and clear it up." Barbara turned and entered the bar area and within a minute a waiter came out with a dustpan and brush. Barbara placed the food order and noticed two men rush from the Reception area in the direction of the toilets. She moved from the bar and followed. The outer door of the gents' toilets had been propped open and Barbara could see Colin sitting on a chair supported by three men.

Moving to the open door she called in. "He's a friend. He's with us. Is he alright? He was a little dizzy outside."

The three faces turned but Colin's chin remained on his chest.

"We've requested an ambulance. Please go to Reception and pass on any personal details you have for him. It will save valuable time when the paramedics arrive."

Barbara moved quickly for a lady of her age but rather than going directly to Reception she popped outside first.

"Colin's collapsed. They're getting an ambulance."

There was silence amongst the group until Melanie spoke. "He's not been well at all. He looked dreadfully pale and a little grey when I first saw him sitting here. I do hope that he'll be alright. Does anyone have his wife's telephone number?"

Most from the group had lost their appetite after watching the stretcher load Drummond into the ambulance. Joan left soon afterwards with two others. Norma, Melanie and Barbara saw little reason to cancel their order. They had waited long enough. They believed it was a case of overindulgence, as he had said himself.

"A typical man, Norma. Always rushing the pleasures of life for quick gratification," Melanie whispered whilst about to sip her red wine. She then giggled into the glass. "If Joan hadn't been so clumsy, we'd have had a spare glass of white too!"

"Ladies, please. Some respect for an ex-colleague at least." Barbara frowned at them both.

"He was fine at the start but goodness, if you're going to have a bad day, his went from bad to worse very rapidly."

"Harrogate's not a large town but I've not seen Joan Rigby since we finished. Must be fifteen years. You think you'd bump into her occasionally whilst out and about. She's not looking too well, I thought." Barbara moved slightly as the waiter brought their food order.

"We've cancelled one of the meals for your colleague who was taken ill but there's a charge for the other ladies who just left."

Barbara realised the error as they had not in fact ordered his lunch. She remained silent and nodded to the waiter. "That's fine." She took the bill. "We have some money in the group kitty that will cover this. Now, who ordered the fish goujons?"

***

The drive back was uneventful and it was a surprise to Hannah that Owen was snoring lightly as they turned into the car park of their apartment building. It was just like when he was a child. *Age doesn't seem to matter. What does is what's in the heart*, she thought.

***

Joan Rigby lifted the trug and pushed the iron lion away from the greenhouse door, before giving it the usual shove in an effort to close it properly. She had collected more leaves, this time from the small bandicoot tree that grew in the far corner as well as a handful of parsley from one of the pots. She was already chewing some of the parsley as she made her way back into the kitchen. Trixie fussed round her feet. "Peet told me about the magic properties of this herb. I know it's doing me good."

"Our usual visit to town tomorrow if the weather is kind." She tapped the cushion on the chair and the dog obediently jumped and quickly settled. As if a ritual, she put the leaves into the simmering pan of water on the stove and popped on the lid before settling on the next chair. She looked at the remaining pieces of jigsaw.

"Well Trixie, let's start putting faces to the group. We've nearly completed it. If only we could turn back time as easily as putting this puzzle together. Now that would be something."

The pan lid protested as it did most days, causing a sudden hissing and spitting. "I'm coming, just give me a minute."

Chapter Twenty-Three

The video footage from the first venue was played on the large flat screen in an adjacent room to the Incident Room where April was working. Cyril had left April with the journals and come to view the video.

This was the third showing and names were being added to a list of those known. Rigby, Seex and Cooper had all been identified as had Cooper's wife, Ingrid.

"Just pause it there," Cyril requested. "Cooper's wife. She seems animated and quite the bon vivant. I know she was at the second meeting but I didn't know she attended this one. But obviously she did. There appears to be no rancour between her and her ex-husband, in fact, it seems from this to be quite the contrary." He jotted a reminder to himself to read April's interview again.

Shakti waited. "We're using some of the LEA's photo records and generally held data from bus pass and drivers' licence images to help identify others. It's painstaking work."

She started the video again and as she did Nixon popped his face round the door. "Colin Drummond, he was on the list as a possible victim, was taken ill at an impromptu meeting of some of the same group. They met at a hotel. He's in critical care. The hospital was immediately alerted to the possibility it might be poisoning and the doctors were able to act accordingly. The swift, medical intervention might just save his life."

Shakti paused the video as both she and Cyril stood.

"Who else was there?" Cyril's question was direct.

Nixon let the door close as he came in. He referred to his notes. "Melanie Masters, Norma Halsall, Barbara Burton, strangely enough, Joan Rigby. According to the first reports she shouldn't have been there. A chance meeting in town had brought her to the venue with two of the other members. Her son was there too, from all accounts."

Cyril immediately looked at Nixon and then Shakti. "Her son? Please, explain!"

"I don't know if I can. It seems Joan shouldn't have been there and neither should her son. Well, he should have been at the hotel as there was a conference linked to educational resources taking place and he was one of the attendees. Apparently, he accidentally bumped into the casualty, Drummond, at the bar, spilling a number of drinks he was carrying. That's Drummond and not Rigby. Anyway, Ian Rigby ordered replacement drinks and took them outside to where they should have been in the first place, which was Drummond's group. He was surprised to see his mother there. Drummond had gone to get cleaned up."

"I think I follow that even though it didn't sound like the Queen's English, Nixon. Let me guess. He didn't return?" Cyril pronounced believing he was ahead of the game.

"No, he did, sir, or should that be yes? Anyway, he came back and seemed alright apart from being covered in red wine. It was only a little later that he had the dizzy spell. From this report, Barbara Burton suggested he was fine. Quite chatty. About fifteen minutes later when he stood to go to the bathroom, he told those present that he felt dizzy. He suggested he'd maybe drunk his first glass of white wine too quickly or that it was his low blood pressure. According to the hospital report he was on certain medication that could cause this."

"What do we know about the conference?"

"*IT and Computer Science in Education* is the title of the event. It was organised for the full day with 124 people attending from around the north east. Began at 09.30 and runs until 17.00. There were a number of suppliers presenting their hardware and software. It's not unusual, conferences are what this town is famous for. It was probably just a coincidence that he bumped into one of the group members, and when I say bumped ..."

Cyril quickly left the room. "A minute!" Returning he held a clipboard containing a collection of sheets. "The list from the Incident Room. Something's nagging me."

He flicked through the pages until he found the one which listed the members of the Pedagogues' Place Facebook group.

"Rigby's mother, here, look. My memory is still serving me correctly. She was not a friend of the Facebook group." His finger ran down the list. "No, she's not here. John Rigby was but not her. Her son, if you recall, set him up on his laptop. He spoke with Owen when he came into the station. Teaching IT and Technology is obviously his forte. I'd like to chat with Ian Rigby and I'd like to chat to him today. Nixon, if you'd be so kind as to organise that, possibly after the conference at the hotel. We'll go there unless he has a strong desire to come here. We have his details from his last visit. I also want any CCTV footage of the incidents that took place there ASAP and I'd like to view it before I speak to Rigby. You know the time scale so an edited version, please."

"Joan Rigby. Do you need to see her?" Nixon asked as he held the door open.

"Not as yet. Let's view the evidence first. I don't like coincidences and I certainly don't like them so close to murder cases."

Nixon left and those watching the video settled back down.

It was twelve minutes later when Cyril Bennett left the Incident Room after issuing instructions to identify everyone within the video seen in the room the group had booked. He knew the task was unlikely to reap any benefits but it was important they try.

April was still ploughing through the journals. Cyril hung up the clipboard. "Did you hear about Drummond?"

"Nixon popped in looking for you. Yes, he told me. I've been looking more closely at these planting diagrams. Two of the plants identified in all the deaths, Oleander and Yew, were designed to go in Rigby's garden, a few varieties of Oleander, mind." She slid the journal holding the garden layout across the table to Cyril.

"You mentioned that these could be in any English garden. What do we know about the other gardens he designed?"

"In there too. He was a great fan of both species but particularly the Yew. In his notes he suggests that you are planting for the future when planting Yew. He also seemed to include a wild flower area. That could mean anything but it might mean Monkshood."

"You reported the garden was overgrown. Do we know why?" Cyril pushed the journal back.

"She told me she'd not been too well recently and to be honest she seemed older than her years."

***

Owen received the letter late in the morning when he returned to his desk. It had been propped against the damaged mug that held his sweets, clearly visible over the layers of papers and files that littered the surface. He did not recognise the writing. It was unusual to receive a letter with the address handwritten and there was no stamp. *Delivered by hand, 09.12,* followed by an abbreviated date had been added in red ink. He had spent most of the morning checking progress with the two known dealers – there had been none to date – and liaising with the Youth Justice Manager. Martin had been granted leave of absence from school with a gradual return programme in place, pending the legal outcome of any offences.

Picking up the envelope he slid the tip of his biro into the top and sliced it open. He sat back.

Dear Detective Inspector Owen,

I wanted to thank you when I left you yesterday to go to my nan's house, but somehow, I was worried about how things were going to be. I probably shouldn't have worried. I was always good at writing essays and factual stuff at school but I found writing this hard, not because I didn't know what I wanted to say, but whether it was right for me to contact you. Mum doesn't know I've written it. Grandad said he'd drop it in.

After Mum chatted with Donna, the lady who was there,

she's been much better. She's stopped worrying, I think and I know she's not cried since we got here. A bit at first but then nothing.

I know I've been a fool and I know also that I've been lucky. I think because of Dad dying I wanted to be compensated. I miss him a lot and it still hurts. I know this wouldn't have happened if he'd been alive. This is the best way I can say this. Thank you for your help and understanding. I like you very much and for a big man you're very kind, gentle and understanding. According to my friends the police don't care, but I now know that's not true and I will tell them if they say differently.

If you meant what you said about being there for me if I ever needed to talk, you said man to man, well it might be boy to man, then I'd like that. I'll not bother you with silly things but I now know that if I'd had that a few months back I'd still be the son my mum loved and was once proud of. I'll keep the number you gave me safe.

I'll see you in the next few days when we know what's going to happen. I did wrong and will take the rap.

I just wanted to say thanks for helping Mum and me. I'll never forget it.

Your friend,
Martin.

Owen read it through a second time before tossing the letter onto the desk. He breathed out slowly. In all his time in the force, at that moment, he felt as though he had achieved something positive and worthwhile. "You're welcome, young man. We all need a helping hand along this path we walk in life. I had many and I'm happy to offer you mine," he vowed loudly.

"Talking to me, Owen?" Smirthwaite's head appeared from behind a computer screen.

Owen took the letter over. "You know the lad I've been dealing with? He can't be all that bad."

Handing over the letter, Smirthwaite read it and then whistled long and low. "Bloody hell. That takes balls to write something like that at his age. I think you might have helped someone dodge a bullet there, Owen. Well done you! Makes the other sad parts of this job just a little more palatable. Whenever you want to give up and throw in the towel, just take that out and read it."

Putting it back in the envelope, Owen tucked it into his pocket.

Chapter Twenty-Four

Cyril had brought in the team to watch the CCTV footage taken from the hotel. Three different cameras covered the areas of the bar, the outside and the corridor leading from the Reception and bar area to the gents' washroom. The technical people had kept them running as if it were a triptych showing the interaction between the areas. They had also edited the footage to begin when Colin Drummond appeared after walking up the drive. The whole thing, from his first appearance to his entering the building before collapsing in the toilets, lasted twenty-four minutes. They watched it once through without interruption. Each made notes.

"Anything?" Cyril moved his chair to the other side of the table, his back to the screen.

"Interesting to see when he was outside at first, he spoke to a woman who was sitting on her own, not with his group. When he went in, she moved over and stood by the table on which he'd placed his drink. She left her newspaper. Just before he returned, she went and sat back down briefly and then left. Had quite a conversation. We only see her back." Smirthwaite was the first to speak.

"Brian, get them to hold CCTV of the Mercer Gallery area and along Crescent Road to Parliament Street. There are cameras at the junction." Cyril squinted at the time markings on screen. "From 11.55 until 12.30. Give them a description." Brian moved to a phone and called Control.

"We know everyone apart from the two who came after Joan Rigby's trio," April announced.

"Which is Joan?" Cyril asked turning to see the screen.

"She has her back to you. She's the one with the small dog."

"That was Ian Rigby you saw coming up the corridor," Owen pointed out. "That was some collision but it doesn't appear to have been contrived."

They continued watching the whole thing again, pausing at intervals.

"Pause it, please." Cyril looked intently. "Did you see that? Joan Rigby has knocked over Drummond's glass. How much wine did he drink from that second glass? Wind it back."

They watched as he returned after cleaning himself up.

Owen started to count out loud the number of times the glass was lifted to his lips as he watched.

"That's one, two and a third, four. The glass is half-full when he leaves."

"Optimist!" April turned and smiled.

"One and a half glasses in twenty minutes." Cyril looked round. "Excessive? Enough to make a grown man dizzy? I think not."

"An elderly man with underlying health issues to be fully accurate."

"So, if we believe he was poisoned then who slipped the Mickey Finn into the wine?" Nixon asked, ever the practical officer. "It wasn't Joan Rigby or any of the other ladies around the table. I've watched them with great interest. Rigby touched it when she knocked it over but at no other time. That's it."

"Why did her son put the tray down just after he left the bar? Again, the camera cannot see the tray or his hands. That's clearly chance number one and as far as I can see, that's the only opportunity if it went in his drink." Owen sat back. "Unless it was in his first. Again, we lost sight of that when she came over to deliver the paper."

Cyril looked at his watch. It was 4.55. "Owen, call the hotel and get them to confirm Ian Rigby knows to wait there after the conference. We're going to see him in a minute or two. April, take someone and visit his mother. I need to find out how she got involved and what she knows. Briefing at 8 tomorrow, Shakti, if you'll sort that. Did we find out if there was ever a legal complaint against any of those three, Seex, Rigby and Cooper?"

"I don't think so but I'll check."

***

On arriving at the hotel, Cyril assessed the area where the group had met. There were now four chairs around each outside table and the umbrellas to three had been folded. He checked the position of the security cameras, walking towards them to look back on the scene as he had witnessed it from the recording. The one other camera was positioned with that of the first but pointing towards the other end of the hotel's frontage. On inspecting the table, Cyril noticed that the minute shards of glass were still visible on the floor.

Ian Rigby was sitting in the bar area reading, a tray of coffee set on a low table before him along with a number of brochures, presumably from the day's conference. He looked up as only Owen entered. Recognising him from their first meeting he stood.

"Inspector Owen." He put out a hand.

Owen shook it.

Rigby looked specifically at his collar but on this occasion it was straight. "What's this about? I'm assuming this lunchtime's incident."

Cyril had gone to see the manager to inform him of the informal interview taking place on his premises, but also with a view to ask about the mystery lady who had ordered coffee outside. He also requested that the newspapers that were found on any outside table be retained. He would collect them later. He soon joined Owen and after introductions the interview started.

***

April and Nixon stopped on the road outside the cottage. She had deliberately not forewarned the woman of their arrival. The front of the cottage was now in shadow. Nixon moved towards the corner and tried the gate set in the stone arch but it was secure. April knocked. Within minutes the lacy curtains covering the window to the right of the door twitched tentatively and then opened as Joan Rigby's face appeared. She smiled and held up her finger as if indicating to wait a moment.

"Goodness, Inspector. I thought it might have been Ian. He said he'd call on his way home. I've made a cheese and ham pie, it's a favourite of his. I use tarragon from the garden. Helps bring out the flavours so well. Come in."

The hallway was dark and they were shown into the lounge. The smell of the cooking had permeated the room giving the cottage a warm and homely feel. Like the garden and the front of the building, there was a sense of neglect. It was not untidy, just missing that final touch. A peace lily and a dragon tree stood by the window. It was clear that they were well cared for.

"You've come about poor Colin, haven't you? I do hope it's not bad news."

"He's not well, Mrs Rigby, but they believe he'll make a full recovery. You were not a member of the group but you were present."

"It was a chance meeting. I wouldn't thank you to sit and go over old times but it was good to see some of them again. I bumped into Norma Halsall and Melanie ... For the life of me I can't remember her surname. Not seen them for years. In teaching, you learn names rapidly but then forget them as more come along to fill the space up here." She tapped the side of her head. "Gets worse the older you get too. Norma and I worked together for a short time in a school in Ripon. In those early days, we moved for promotion if we could. Sometimes as you came in others would be going out."

"The meeting?" April asked urging the conversation to move forward.

"Sorry, yes. I was coming from the old Pump Room, and they were just walking towards the crossing. I can't tell you how many years it's been since we met but it's a fair few. They were late for the meeting and invited me along. Can you believe I saw Ian, my son, there too? Serendipity, really. I knew many of the people attending from another lifetime. I thought I'd met Colin before but I couldn't remember him, only his sharp facial features rang a bell. He assured me we'd met at the Teachers' Centre and although his face seemed familiar, I couldn't recall. I think I upset him by saying that. Anyway, we'd just ordered food and then it was spoiled in a way by Colin's illness. I didn't stay after that."

"You just left?" Nixon asked, knowing what had occurred from watching the video.

"I left with Pippa and Carole. To be honest it disturbed me. You see, Inspector Richmond, I've been poorly these last few months. The news is not very positive, unfortunately, and there's little they can do. I've refused some specialist treatments. I've had a good life and I don't want to be a burden on anyone."

Nixon looked at April.

"Please come with me. Trixie will make a fuss but she'll soon calm down if you ignore her. I spoil her far too much." Joan stood and went through the kitchen into the garden, following the path to the greenhouse. Trixie followed running and jumping at Nixon's legs. He did as he was asked and ignored the dog. It quickly tired and returned to the kitchen. Tugging the door brought a rattle to the surrounding glass. Nixon instinctively ducked thinking something was about to collapse. Rigby giggled before sliding the iron lion with her foot to prop the door open. She went in. The trapped warmth of the late sun was immediately felt; even through the unwashed glass the temperature had built.

"Ignore the tomatoes, they're well past their best and will not be allowed to ripen. I will use them as they are. They have certain special medicinal properties when eaten like that. Now see here, this is what I've brought you to look at." She pointed to numerous pots that were set on a long, wooden trellis table. "Herbs, medicinal herbs as I guess all herbs are. These, however, are different. This is *Leea indica* or bandicoot, the berry is what you need but the leaf is good too, *Vitex trifolia* or simpleleaf such a clever plant and my favourite if only for the name, *Clausena lansium* or fool's curry leaf."

"I don't fully understand."

"Homeopathy. I decided to treat myself using the recipes and medicines from the past."

Nixon let his foot touch April's as if expressing his disbelief. This is not what they had come for. April was unsure as to how to get the interview back on track without seeming callous and insensitive, but time was pressing. "Mrs Rigby, may I ask if you saw anyone touch or tamper with Mr Drummond's drink?"

She immediately flushed red. "Me!" She held her hands up as if April were pointing a gun at her.

Chapter Twenty-Five

Ian Rigby was totally at ease with all of the questions. He explained the bar room accident and how he had never met Drummond. He added that seeing his mother sitting outside with the same group had come as a bit of a shock.

"We've not seen eye to eye since her diagnosis. She has cancer. They said it was advanced as she'd kept the symptoms to herself for far too long. The prognosis was poor. She'd decided, in some kind of warped wisdom, that she'd research homeopathy cures and the medicines of the ancients and treat herself." He shook his head. "Ever tried communicating with a stubborn parent of the female variety? She just wouldn't listen. She batted away logic with mysticism and I found I could neither argue with her nor make her see sense. When I said she was selfish, she levelled the same argument straight back. It was me. She said if I truly loved her, I'd support her along this chosen path of hers. Can you see a logic? I can't. It's just bloody bonkers. She'd rather see a Druid than a doctor!"

Cyril immediately thought of his own mother and how she too had resigned herself bravely knowing she had a terminal condition. In some small way he understood.

"I did everything I could to persuade her from her chosen medicinal path but she told me that she had notes and a book given to her by the chap that helped with the garden. Mr Peet, great name for a gardener, just the wrong spelling. Sorry!" He put his hands behind his head and stretched, a gesture demonstrating his pure frustration. "She told me that Peet had been into self-help and nature's healing pathways – as if that was going to change my mind. I told her that he died and didn't live to a great old age despite his wisdom. He had demonstrated to her how to extract the goodness and medicinal properties from plants, from the leaves, the roots and the stems and with her scientific knowledge she soon became hooked. Have you tried camomile tea?" He paused looking at both men before him and saw both heads move, as if by instinct, from side to side in concert. "I thought not. Homemade too. You never want to, believe me. Peet drank and chewed all sorts of weird crap. I kid you not. I worked with him on Mum's garden. Always called me Fellow-me-lad or young lad, never Ian. He talked about nature's healers and nature's killers and how each could be harnessed to serve. He was a bloody good gardener. Said he owed his strength, fit mind and his health to eating what he grew. The taking of medicinal herbs in various ways on a regular basis was the key. Reminded me of a hippy the way he spoke, what with flower power and all that. Peace!"

"Nature's killers? Did he say more?" Owen asked moving closer to the coffee table.

"Yes. We'd chat over a brew and he'd show me the shrubs he'd planted that were poisonous. Made me scared to touch some of them and he knew which always made him chuckle. I remember he particularly loved the yew tree. Did you know that every part of it is poisonous apart, that is, from the flesh of the berry? That, according to Peet, is the sweetest fruit of all fruits. I took his word for it. There's a lot of poison in the small stone in the centre but you spit that out he assured me. Trouble with the yew, it takes an age to grow. He was a delightful old chap. Weird but lovely. A different generation from a different era."

Cyril needed to return to the event.

"Why, after you'd collected the drinks, did you stop and put the tray on the table before going outside?"

"One of the glasses wasn't on the small paper mat correctly. I'd already lost one set of drinks and I certainly didn't want to lose another. I stopped to adjust it. Hell, I nearly dropped them when I saw Mum." He looked at his watch. "I'm going there after this. She's probably slaughtered the fatted calf as she does in her own inimitable way."

"One last question. You set your father up on the Facebook page and dealt with the early communications which means you knew his passwords and could check remotely on his progress?"

"Yes, it's what I teach."

"Have you been on without his knowledge at any time before or after your father's death, just to see what was going on? Curiosity after all is a human trait when we care about someone."

Rigby leaned back and immediately folded his arms. Both Cyril and Owen interpreted the swift change in body language. The barriers had been raised.

"Yes, just to make sure he wasn't making a fool of himself. You know of his reputation. He didn't change and neither did the others."

"They posted pictures from their past. Some had their own image as their profile picture. Did your father?"

"You know he did."

"And Colin Drummond? What about Colin, Mr Rigby. Have you ever seen a photograph of him?"

Rigby nodded his head.

"Owen."

Owen immediately cautioned Rigby. "You are not under arrest but ..." He went through the caution statement. "Do you understand that means you speak and not nod as gestures cannot be interpreted accurately."

Cyril immediately asked the same question again. "Have you seen a photograph of Colin Drummond?"

"I've seen one when he was a young teacher standing alongside a group of people, I assumed they were colleagues. My father and mother were on the photograph. I've seen his profile image too, yes. I hovered the cursor over the photograph and as you're aware names can come up of those in the group. His did."

"Seex and Cooper also?"

He was about to nod again but quickly responded in the affirmative. "It was early, before my parents married. She was down as Nicholson, her maiden name."

Cyril frowned. He had heard that name before but he could not recall where. He grabbed a piece of paper from the table. "May I?"

"Be my guest. It belongs to the hotel. There's a pen there somewhere under one of the pamphlets."

Cyril found it and made a note before folding it and popping it into his jacket pocket. He stopped himself from taking the pen.

"I can assure you, Detective Inspector Bennett, I have done nothing wrong."

"Chief Inspector. This is a serious crime, Mr Rigby, so we have senior police officers working the case. We are looking for a serial killer who continues to try and kill for whatever reason and strangely, they're using a weapon you know quite a lot about. You will be allowed to visit your mother this evening but I'll need you at the station tomorrow morning. You'll be able to arrange that otherwise we'll take you there this evening."

"Yes, I can phone my headteacher now. I've a light day tomorrow, it should be easily covered."

"Have you ever been married, Mr Rigby?"

"Is such a personal question of relevance?"

Cyril said nothing, he just waited. He knew Rigby would either tell him or tell him to bugger off.

Rigby shook his head. "If you'd witnessed what I had, a father who enjoyed to play strange marital games, it does things to you, harms you emotionally when you're young and impressionable. It certainly makes you question whether marriage is the right path."

Cyril understood exactly and moved the questioning on.

"One last thing. Did you go outside before this incident, before they arrived? You'd been there since … What time?"

"Nine. Yes." From his pocket he withdrew an electronic cigarette. "I'm a slave to this."

The more he talked, the more Cyril felt as though he had a soulmate.

"Did you go out about 10.30, maybe a coffee break?"

"Yes. With a coffee."

"Did anyone else?"

"A teacher from Hull, a woman, a smoker, she came with me. We chatted."

"Was there anyone at the tables?"

"There was a woman sitting on the first table to the right of the door. She was reading a paper, a broadsheet. I went to ask if I could have the ashtray that was there. I took it as she wasn't smoking."

"Had you seen her before?"

"No. We were there only briefly. If I saw her again, I might recognise her but I can't say honestly that I'd seen her before."

Cyril stood. "This will be the last question. "When did you last see your father?"

Rigby laughed. "A famous painting that hung on many a primary school wall. William Frederick Yeames, if my memory serves me correctly, a British painter. Depicts a young lad being questioned by the Parliamentarians, appropriate, don't you think? The last time? He'd broken two teeth eating an almond. It caused him quite a bit of distress. I saw him a couple of times during his treatment. He had one extracted. I believe it was his first too." He looked again at his watch. "That was the third last question. Do you have more or can I go?"

Rigby left as Cyril went to the Reception to speak to the duty manager again. The waiter who served the woman came from the bar area as requested. He could not offer any further assistance but he brought the newspaper. Cyril was assured that the CCTV for the whole of that day would be forwarded once the data controller of the hotel received the official data release request. Cyril made the necessary calls to set the wheels in motion.

Chapter Twenty-Six

April and Harry Nixon continued the interview with Joan Rigby. It was proving difficult to keep her on track.

"I can normally blame the dog when things like that occur, but in all honesty, it was me. I knocked over his glass but he wasn't too bothered about anything other than getting to the bathroom. Thankfully it wasn't full, the glass and not the bathroom you understand." She giggled. "Sorry, I can be an old fool. I shouldn't laugh. The poor man!"

Nixon helped close the greenhouse door. It was more difficult than he had anticipated.

"You need to get your son to shave some off that, must get worse in winter." Nixon inspected the fragile framework before following the ladies up the pathway. How it had remained standing he would never know.

"It'll not be used by then, winter, I can assure you of that, Mr Nixon. I can definitely guarantee that!"

Entering the kitchen, Trixie leapt from her bed and skipped across the room.

"Not now Trixie. Come on through to the lounge, it's more comfortable there."

Nixon, the last to enter, took a moment to make a fuss of the dog. She curled round his legs before rolling over and spread her paws aloft, eagerly seeking a kind hand.

"She'll stand that all day. She loves a fuss. Doesn't like Ian, my son, the milkman or the postman, tends to prefer the ladies. Funny is our Trixie, she seems to only take to certain men. You're one of the privileged few, Mr Nixon. Now leave the poor man be, Trixie, he has work to do."

Joan had only briefly turned before continuing towards the front room. April followed. Nixon stopped to respond to the dog's demands. He stroked her chest briefly but realised he could, as she had warned, be there all day. Standing, the dog rolled back onto four legs, stood and shook herself. Nixon followed the others only to stop at the table containing the two trays. He studied the puzzle and then the remaining pieces spread around the first tray. Collecting a piece, he placed it into the jigsaw with a tap of the finger. A guilty smile came to his lips before he made his way to the lounge.

"How long have you known about the disease, Mrs Rigby?"

"You know when things aren't right and you think it will pass. We've all been there and then … it doesn't. It grows worse and then a nagging fear creeps into your mind. A year, maybe more. I never liked visiting the doctor but I did. I had the tests, camera both up and down. They confirmed it then and for a short time my life stopped being my own."

"Treatments?"

"Yes. Visits here and visits there. Ian was so generous with his time and another friend helped too. It was then that I made my decision. I'd been controlled too much in my past with John and I certainly wasn't going to be controlled again, not at my age. I'd always taken an interest in plant medicines and they'd looked after me in the past or at least I believe they had. In life, when faced with crossroads, one has to make decisions. Many people would follow the doctors and the specialists. I didn't."

"The path less trodden?" April added.

"If you say so. We're all destined to follow the final pathways, Inspector Richmond, but do remember that there's only one ultimate destination. We will all arrive there at some point. Look at John. What do they also say? You reap what you sow?"

April glanced at Nixon and then stood. "Thank you very much."

"I'm sorry, forgive me, I didn't offer you a drink."

April smiled. "You have been more than generous with your time, thank you. Besides, you told us your son was going to call."

April and Nixon sat in the car conscious that Rigby was watching through the lacy curtains. "Fancy a coffee and a debrief?"

Nixon nodded. "Did you see the puzzle on the tray in the kitchen? Looked like one of those you can have professionally made from a photograph. I'd say it was of a collection of young teachers. What is it about that profession that makes them stand out from the rest?"

"Leather patches on their jacket sleeves?"

"Funny thing was, April, all the faces were missing, well most. The rest of the puzzle was completed. The pieces with the faces were in the second tray. Don't tell more than six people but I couldn't resist popping one of the pieces in!" He turned and grinned. "See, I can be wicked when I want to be. I'm just like the rest; pure evil underneath!"

Nixon came out of the Westminster Arcade carrying two coffees from the tea room on the upper floor. April had parked on the narrow back road. The coffee smelled good and the additional cardboard that was wrapped round the cup was warm.

"Impressions of Mrs Rigby, Harry?"

"Brave woman. Hell, I'd have all the treatment they'd be prepared to throw at me. You women can be tough cookies, especially the older you get. My mother was very similar in her general outlook. I remember once she stood up suddenly whilst cleaning a kitchen cupboard and banged her head. I thought I could see her brains as there was so much blood. She told me to stop fussing and get a towel. She never had it looked at. She was cleaning again within the hour."

"It was something she said just as we were leaving."

"'You reap what you sow'," he immediately answered before sipping more coffee. "Those words hit me straight away. Then *Cluedo* came to mind. I can see that we could have the *who* and we have a possible *with what,* it's the *why,* particularly when I'm thinking about Seex and Cooper. I could understand her poisoning her own husband, he sounded a right prat, but Cooper? He'd been a friend of the family for some time."

"What happens amongst families usually stays amongst them, the bad, at any rate. The good gets broadcast. If you've ever received one of those bloody awful round robin letters at Christmas, you'd know just what I mean. I'm wondering if she'd been involved with either Seex or Cooper when she moved out on her own. Young woman, living the life of a nun, two sexual predators whom she knows and more importantly, they know her. Convenient? Did she get promotion, help with going part time, a cushy job to help her spend more time at home? I'm just thinking out loud, as a woman is allowed to do!"

***

Ian Rigby parked on the road outside his mother's cottage and for a moment he reflected on the day. He could never have predicted the course of events that led to this moment. The last few months had been strange, what with the diagnosis and then his father's death.

The cottage door opened and he was greeted with a growl from Trixie and a smile from his mother. He leaned forward and kissed her as the dog snapped at his trouser leg. He flicked her with his foot.

"Only place in the world where your lips are kissed and your arse gets bitten."

She picked up Trixie who continued to bare her teeth until Joan slapped her across the snout, more in show than anger. "You just leave my lovely boy alone, you're just jealous."

She put the dog in the lounge and closed the door. "I've made you your favourite meal. I'm hungry as I didn't eat this lunchtime."

"I wasn't hungry, Mum, until I smelled the cooking. Cheese and ham if I'm not mistaken? Thank you."

Entering the kitchen, she collected the two trays from the table quickly slotting one onto the other.

"Set the table, there's a love. I'll just pop these in the lounge."

Ian heard his mother talking to the dog. On returning she checked the oven. "It's on tick over. You just say when you want to eat."

They both sat, she in the comfortable chair, whilst he took one of the carvers. "I was surprised to see you this lunchtime. Thought you had a coffee in the morning and then home."

She went through the explanation she had given to the officers only an hour earlier. "To be honest, Ian, I did feel a little uncomfortable in their company. I don't want them to know of my condition and I know I'm not looking at my best. Some of them would put two and two together and start interrogating, as only teachers can. You should know that yourself. Just think what you can glean when you're trying to extract the truth from a stubborn child. I should have put my foot down, stuck to my guns and said no to their persistent invitations. If I hadn't popped into the sweet shop for that fudge, I'd never have bumped into them."

"The chap, Drummond, he was quite ill. Has he been here, to the house? Do you know him? Was he a teacher?"

His mother said nothing but then nodded. "A drink, dear? That's what we need."

Ian stood and went to the fridge. "You used to keep the odd beer."

"Bottom cupboard by the sink and use a glass."

Flicking the top, Ian took a glass from the draining board, checked it and poured. "You?"

"No, I'll have some herbal tea after my meal. I need to keep to my routine."

"Gin and tonic part of that lunchtime routine?"

"Go on then, a small one seeing I left most of the one I had at lunch. It'll not kill me."

Ian shook his head. "That's so true mother, so true!"

***

Cyril turned the key and pushed open the door. Owen had dropped him off and he was home earlier than he had planned. He collected the mail and quickly checked it. Julie was not home. He needed a coffee. Taking off his shoes, he added water to the coffee machine before putting in a pod. Slipping off his jacket he checked the pockets tossing various items onto the table. From his inner pocket he brought out the folded paper. He opened it. *Nicholson.* Leaving the note open on the kitchen worktop, he continued to clear things away. He made coffee whilst occasionally looking at the name on the sheet. *Where have I heard your name before?*

Hearing the front door open, he collected another cup, added a pod and prepared coffee for Julie.

***

"Yes, I knew him in the past. I knew them all in the past. Past tense, Ian, past tense. That's why I don't go to their dos, don't follow them on social media. Why? Because some things are better forgotten, better, if I dare say it, *buried.*"

"What exactly is going on? Dad, Cooper and Seex, then this poor chap today. I'm your son, I know I'm cross with you because you won't listen to medical reason. I've already lost one parent but that doesn't seem to register with you. Your pigheaded, false hope will no doubt see you follow him. Something's not right, and you're keeping whatever it is from me."

He had just stopped speaking and brought the beer to his lips when there was a crash from the lounge followed by a yelp from Trixie. Ian shot to his feet and opened the door. The two trays were on the floor and a number of pieces were scattered. Trixie sat in the far corner waiting for the wrath of Gods. Joan followed him in. Ian heard her sigh.

The sound was honest and desperate as if her world had come apart too.

"All that work. Trixie, how could you?"

Ian lifted the first tray, moved the few pieces spread on the carpet and then righted the lower one. "It'll be fine. I can save a lot of it. Most is still joined. We'll do it after tea. I'll help you put it back as it was. I'll need some stiff cardboard."

"The stupid dog. I've worked so hard to get the jigsaw to this point. I wanted so much to put the rest together."

"Mother, it's a jigsaw and not a family treasure. It will fix. For goodness sake keep things in perspective. The dog didn't do it on purpose. Go and sort the tea and I'll fix this."

Within minutes he had saved the completed section in six separate pieces and carried the trays back into the kitchen. "See, the world continues to spin. Let's eat and then we can complete this and chat."

***

Cyril poured two glasses of wine. The pizza Julie had brought home was waiting to go into the oven as she prepared the salad. They had talked briefly about their day. Cyril had left the small piece of paper on the worktop.

"Secret lover, Cyril? Phone number already chewed and swallowed when you heard the front door open. I can see where it's been torn from the bottom, you just didn't have time to swallow the name. Nicholson is a long one. Had it been Smith or Jones the evidence would have gone." She turned and watched as he smiled.

"Delusional, simply delusional. Cheers!"

"Have you been liaising with her after your last meeting?"

221

Cyril put down his glass. "What last meeting?" The words came out slowly and quizzically.

"She was the woman who witnessed the accident, gave a brief statement. Seex's accident at the top there. We both read it. You were seriously troubled by seeing the young paramedic's face. Remember?"

"Bloody hell. Julie Bennett, you're a star."

"A delusional star. You sure know how to flatter your wife and lover. Cheers to you too."

Chapter Twenty-Seven

The fog had returned to Harrogate's early morning streets. The Stray seemed to wear the thick blanket with a certain confidence yet an eerie grace. Some figures appeared as if by magic, their blurred outlines gradually coming into full focus, whilst others were swallowed in the same wrapping. *It's an Impressionist's dream*, he thought.

Cyril stood at the end of the passageway looking at the street tables and seating where he had first seen Joan Nicholson. How could he have forgotten that? He had read the report, insignificant as it was. It had been overtaken by more pressing issues, murder in fact. She had seen the crash. Maybe it was the face of the paramedic that had branded an image so impermeably into his mind that the peripheral elements of it all had been bleached white and had somehow been eradicated.

Stepping out between two parked cars he began to cross the road. A car horn sounded to his left. Not looking in that direction, he broke into a run. Everyone was in a rush.

He paused by the wrought iron railings around the standing stone, the same stone that had stopped Seex's car. He read the inscription carved within the gritstone – *BOUNDARY OF THE LEEDS AND RIPON TURNPIKE ROADS.*

What must it have been like living back then when the pace of life was no faster than a horse could run? As this thought drifted in his mind, he allowed his hand to touch the rough stone's ancient surface. It was good to see the fence had been replaced, the speed of the repair immediately contradicting his previous premise. *Efficiency and speed are not necessarily the same thing, Bennett.* He looked down at his shoes, the shine was immaculate as usual. *You need to sharpen up. Forgetting that name would never have happened a few years ago. You're relying on others too much, delegating too many things.* His mood changed as he set off towards the other end of The Stray on the path that would lead onto Otley Road. To anyone watching his progress they would soon see him swallowed up. He would vanish, ghostlike into the grey of the early day.

***

It had been a busy early start as Cyril finished reading the report from April and Nixon's visit to Joan Rigby. It still irked him to think he had not matched her with the woman at the scene of the accident. He closed the file as officers moved to take their seats in the Incident Room.

All eyes were fixed on the large screen as the digital recording was rewound from the moment Colin Drummond had spoken to the mystery woman. Thirty-five minutes previously she had walked up the drive.

"I want it in real time until I say pause, please." Cyril never took his eyes from the screen. "Pause. What's she doing?"

"Checking where the cameras are located from the look of it."

She too had paused and it was clear from the manner in which she surveyed the façade that this was her intention.

"Anyone any clues?" Cyril asked, turning immediately to

April.

"It's Ingrid Cooper, Stan Cooper's wife."

"Are we sure?"

"Positive, sir." She slid another photograph of her towards him.

Cyril observed.

The video was started again. "She didn't enter the hotel, she went immediately to the chosen table, removed a broadsheet and started to read. Within five minutes one of the waiting staff approached. He returned with a tray of coffee."

"She's paid straight away. That allows flexibility when you need to leave."

They were soon back at the point where the previous edited recording had started. They watched again with a greater focus.

"From his expression would you say that they knew each other?" The point where Drummond chatted briefly to the woman was watched repeatedly. His face was directly in front of the camera but all they could see was the back of her head.

"It's difficult to say," April responded. "If we take a short break, I can get someone to help answer that question."

"Coffee if you wish folks. Five minutes and no longer. Owen, thanks. Saucer too and no morse code." Cyril smiled and patted Owen's arm.

"Dot, dot bloody dash."

"Dash, that's the spirit, Owen, as we don't have much time."

April made a call and within ten minutes an officer arrived. "This is Karen, our officer who works with the deaf.

Lip reads perfectly." The video was started and Karen stood, her attention fixed on Drummond's lips.

"'I need to save this table but I need more chairs. Could you be kind enough to watch nobody sits here. I've left my things. Thank you. I'll only be a minute.' That's it. From my experience, the formality of that one-sided conversation would suggest they didn't know each other unless they were playing some sort of game."

"Thank you," April responded. "Please stay and help with the other conversations." Karen smiled and took a seat near the front. She began to jot down words when she could read what was being said.

"The lady is speaking to the one with the dog," Karen explained.

April interrupted. "That's Melanie talking and the one to her right is Norma Halsall."

"The large lady just arriving was either late or missed a bus. She moves her head quickly and frequently. I'd have to study the images in much greater detail to know her exact words," Karen said, turning to April.

"Can you try to get what the man says in reply? It's important," Cyril asked as he moved further forward as they neared the section where Drummond stood. "It's coming up in a second or two."

Karen leaned closer. She started to write shorthand and then translated. "'Sorry, I must have drunk the first wine a little too enthusiastically, either that or my blood pressure has fallen. I need the loo, sorry. Please exc ...' I don't think he finished the sentence."

An officer appeared at the door. "Sir?"

Cyril turned.

"Mr Ian Rigby is waiting downstairs. Shall I show him into an interview room? Cooper is on her way in too, sir. She has, I am informed, been cautioned."

"Good. I'll organise a warrant to search the house and gardens, the gardens particularly," Cyril responded. "Have we heard anything further about Drummond?"

"Improving, thankfully. The stomach contents and blood samples have been sent to Forensic toxicology as well as the hospital lab. Either way, we should soon know what he'd been given." The officer left.

Chapter Twenty-Eight

Owen walked part of the way with Cyril until his phone rang. Seeing the expression on Owen's face, Cyril knew it was serious.

"It's Martin, the lad mixed up with the drugs. They had a link signal from his personal security alarm. Emergency services went to the displayed co-ordinates."

"And?"

"He's been attacked by three youths, stabbed. He's on his way to the hospital. They've only caught one of the kids. Can you believe he's thirteen?"

"From Leeds?"

"Manchester but who knows what story they're told to recite. Could be Timbuktu."

Cyril watched as Owen's head fell to his chest.

"I've let him down, sir."

"Rubbish, you followed procedures. Other than wrap him in cotton wool you could have done no more. Get over to the hospital. Talk to him if you can. Remember, that alarm has probably saved him from more harm."

***

Ian Rigby was sitting in Interview Room Four. An officer had just brought him the water he had requested. Cyril entered.

"Sorry, we don't serve camomile tea here but I'm sure you're grateful for that! The coffee can be even worse at times. I wouldn't thank you for the water either but then ..."

228

He dropped the files onto the desk and took the chair facing Ian. "Thank you for coming in. I have a report from the officers who interviewed your mother yesterday."

Rigby was surprised by Bennett's manner. He expected his approach to be more of an interrogation, that it would have a degree of abruptness that you see on the television police programmes, not a chat about his requested beverage. It made him relax but he remained cautious.

"How was your mother when you arrived there yesterday evening, Mr Rigby?"

"She was fine, certainly not herself but considering all of the circumstances ... It's not every day you have the police round, detectives, serious crime detectives at that. She became totally irrational when a jigsaw she was working on was knocked over by the dog. That's just not like her. You've seen how she deals with the serious matters in life, so a puzzle? Makes no sense. To be honest, I'm worried."

"Yesterday you mentioned you'd seen your father, the last few times when he had the dental issues and therefore just before his death."

"That's the truth."

"I know it is. Did you tell your mother?" The way Cyril phrased the question showed a concern rather than the true reason for asking.

"I can't remember." He paused for a moment. "Yes, yes I did because she immediately gave me the tincture to give to him, a small bottle of cloves or something. Said I had it as a child when I was teething and once when I had dental work after a crunching rugby tackle. It did help. There was not much in the bottle. A couple of days later she said she had a new bottle and could I give it to dad. I did. I called after work. It was the day before he died."

"You're certain your mother gave it to you to give to him?"

"Certain."

Cyril stood. "I'll not be a moment."

Leaving the room, he made a call and waited in the corridor. It took four minutes for the officer to hand over the plastic Forensic envelope containing the bottle found in John Rigby's pocket.

"Would this be the bottle?" Cyril pushed the bag across. "Please leave it in the bag."

"I'd say so but I never really took that much notice."

"Did she give any instructions regarding application?"

"To put some on his finger and apply the finger and therefore the tincture directly into the cavity where the tooth had been extracted."

"Anything else?"

Rigby sat back. There was a considerable silence but Cyril knew he was replaying his mother's instructions back through his mind. There came a moment where Rigby's eyes fell on Cyril's and both men stared at each other. Suddenly there was a mutual understanding, a realisation of the truth. Cyril held up his hand as Rigby was about to speak.

"I know, Mr Rigby, you're only guilty in these murders of trying to be a loyal son. Let me get that out of the way. It was confirmed to me yesterday when we chatted in the hotel. Your mother told you under no circumstances were you to try the tincture. Am I correct?"

Rigby's facial expression told Cyril he had hit the bull's eye.

"Not in those words, but yes, you're right. She also said he could use it as a mouthwash if the gum was really painful and it was safe to swallow."

"Now, the next thing. Did you talk to your mother about the Facebook Group, the one you were surreptitiously monitoring after you shouldn't have been?"

He nodded before answering. "Yes, I told her a few things and then she kept asking."

"In your first interview with my colleague, you mentioned a few names. You mentioned a Joan but you said there was never a surname and that she wasn't a friend of the group. There was no one listed by the name of Joan."

"That's right. Seex was always banging on about meeting up with either someone called Joan or he added a simple 'J'. He received a bit of ribbing but it was clear he wasn't liked. You can understand that from the comments. They don't say 'you're a prat' but there's an implication. He must have seen it too if he had any sense."

"Could that have been your mother, the mystery woman?"

***

Owen noticed the officer sitting outside Martin's room. He tapped on the door and entered. To his relief, Martin was sitting up in bed. His mother and grandfather were with him. His face lit up as Owen entered and then he broke down in tears.

"You can stop that! Only called to check on you. Had me worried, my young friend." Owen tousled his hair. "Right, what went down?"

"I'd seen the car and knew that things weren't right. You said if in doubt shout, right?"

Owen nodded.

"It had passed me twice and each time it had slowed and then set off again. When I saw it the third time, I pressed the alarm. It was then I saw them get out. Three, I think. The car shot off, so did I but I tried to jump a fence to get into someone's front garden and I fell. They were about my age. I felt one hit me, like a punch but I saw that he'd stabbed me in the leg and then I heard the siren. They did too. A bloke whose garden it was came out of the house and grabbed one. The other two ran off. That bloke just wrapped him up. He was quick. I then saw the three knives on the floor. They'd dropped them in their hurry to go. The alarm. It worked."

"You worked, you were vigilant and did the right thing. Goodness you had me worried. Hopefully we'll get something from the one that's in our custody. He'll not take the rap for the others that's for sure. We have our ways. I'm proud of you, Martin Dawson. So very proud." Owen put out his hand and Martin shook it. There was a strength to Martin's grip that was missing the first time they had met. "You have my number. Ring me when you're home and I'll pop round and see you."

As Owen reached the door Martin called after him. "Will they come again? Tell me they won't."

Returning to the bed, Owen sat. He could see fear in Martin's eyes and in his mother's. "When I was your age, I was bigger than the other kids in school, I think I was the tallest but I was also broad. I played on the rugby team. Outside school I was picked on, not because I was weak, but because I was a challenge. I became the lad you had a pop at. In many ways the big lad was bullied but I couldn't show that and I accepted those challenges. Later it became two against me as they couldn't beat me on their own. It was then, Martin, that I learned something. To talk about it. To tell someone wiser. I was good with my fists and feet but suddenly I became stronger, not because I lifted weights and stuff, but because I learned ways to defuse situations. I could read what was about to happen just like you did. You get this sixth sense when something isn't right and you put the precautions that you've taken into action. Do you understand what I'm saying?"

Martin nodded.

"There are no promises in life, Martin. I can't be honest with you and then tell you it won't happen again. I'd be lying if I did. What I can do is give you a sword and a shield, surround you with people who will help if you ask. The alarm is there for as long as you need it. We'll be working hard to bring not only those who attacked you, but those who tricked you in the first place, to justice. The lads who attacked you are just like you were. They're lost, believing they're flying when in fact they are falling, spiralling out of control until they crash to the ground. You, Martin and only you, saved yourself. Some are not that strong. Walk tall, keep vigilant and never be afraid to talk and ask for help. I did and in no way am I a weak or cowardly person." Owen did not smile he simply stared at his young friend. "You can count on me. You know where I am."

***

Ingrid Cooper sat silently in the back of the police car. She looked straight ahead. It had been the same when she had been cautioned. Her partner had made a fuss demanding to know what was going on. When the police refused to commit, he demanded an answer from Ingrid. None came. The car containing the search team brought even greater consternation. He went with her.

Chapter Twenty-Nine

Ian sipped the water. "Anything's possible but you'd have to stretch your disbelief a long way. I really couldn't say. She's never talked about another man other than the guy, Peet, the gardener and health guru."

"Did she ever talk about Cooper's wife?"

"Ingrid? Another name from the past. Not a usual Yorkshire name, Inspector. More recently when I've called, she did crop up in the conversation what with her husband dying too."

"What's interesting, and you must see this from my perspective, that of a policeman, is that the evidence shows that they both died from the same thing. Poisoning. I should say both murdered. We know that your father was killed by that tincture we talked about. Interesting poison in that. Monkshood, has a Latin name but for the life of me I can't recall it. That's why you were specifically instructed by your mother not to take it. Had you done so, you would be in the morgue and not here. Maybe not, as you're younger and without, I assume, underlying health conditions. You'd have been ill and she didn't want that."

"Are you telling me my mother killed my father?"

"I am. I have the evidence you see. I have the who, the with what and the why. She also killed Seex, but I just need a few more pointers, more clues you might say. This case is like one of your mother's jigsaw puzzles. It's only when the pieces come together do we see the whole picture. I wonder whose heads were missing from that puzzle the dog knocked over? The puzzle might be a clue just like the glass that was knocked over at the hotel. What did that contain?"

Ian stared at Cyril. "There didn't appear to be anything other than wine when I took it out to them."

"You're right, of course. There was nothing. It was knocked over deliberately, let's say as a precautionary act as your mother did not expect to be discovered. Did you tell your mother that there was a meeting planned yesterday, just let it slip?"

"When I rang her, probably, yes."

"You knew she has coffee in town most mornings. Not every morning. Did you know that on some of those occasions she would meet Seex?"

Ian frowned. "Seex?"

"We showed his photograph to the staff at the coffee shop and they confirmed it was Seex. The day he died he not only drank coffee but had eaten breakfast too. Now if your mother can make a tincture of such strength that a few finger dabs causes the death of a man with a poor heart, what could she slip into coffee and breakfast? After all, Seex was another of the walking wounded, so what could she have used? What's worse, he crashed his car soon afterwards and, unbelievably, right in front of her. She could not have planned that, of course, and neither could she have foreseen that he'd kill a young mother crossing the road that very morning – but he did. You might even say, she did!"

Rigby just stared at Cyril. "Bloody hell. I'm so sorry. I

read about that. My mother?"

"How and where did she make these things? That's the question, Mr Rigby. That's the million-dollar question."

***

A female officer stood by the door and Ingrid, arms folded, maintained her silence. She had refused legal representation so the duty solicitor had been requested. She also rejected the opportunity to have her partner present. April and Nixon monitored the room using the CCTV. Neither had known anyone remain mute from the start of an arrest.

DC Henry Jones appeared carrying an electronic tablet. "Thought you should see this, ma'am, before you interview the suspect."

April and Nixon watched the recording as the camera panned the interior of what appeared to be a shed. They listened to the accompanying commentary from Forensics. It paused on the bicycle propped against what appeared to be an old, school lab bench.

The camera focused briefly on the tyre.

We've run a check and the tyre matches the markings found at Cooper's murder site. Dirt samples have been taken.

The camera panned to one of the shelves and again focused on three bottles, chemistry flasks.

It would appear that the bench and these flasks have recently been handled if we compare some of the items on the same shelf. There is also a camping burner, a pan and other equipment that might have been used in the extraction of poison from plants.

"Methanol, Benzine and Chloroform," Nixon read.

237

They continued to watch as the camera zoomed in on a ball of paper nestling on a pile of boxes in a corner.

This paper looks relatively new. It has been extensively photographed in situ.

They observed as it was retrieved and a gloved hand carefully unfolded the sheet.

"Well, would you look at that! Takes me back to my school chemistry homework." Nixon leaned closer to the screen. "Crystallisation. Bingo!"

April turned to the officer. "Has Bennett seen this evidence?"

"No, It's new. It was directed to you as SIO."

"Please make sure he sees it ASAP."

***

"I'm about to do something most unusual, Mr Rigby," Cyril remarked. "I'm going to ask you to come with me to interview your mother. You now know the situation. It's not standard police procedure but then this isn't a standard case and considering her general health ..."

"That's fine. Anything I can do."

As they left the Interview Room the officer with the tablet approached.

"Inspector Richmond would like you to see this. It's a matter of urgency, sir."

Cyril requested she take Rigby to sit in the interview lounge and get him a coffee whilst he checked the information. Once done, he went along to watch April's interview on screen. Nixon was in the room.

"Nothing so far, sir. She hasn't said a word since we arrived at the house."

"She will. She'll speak with you or the solicitor when she

needs something. The call of nature will ensure that."

Chapter Thirty

The driver pulled up outside the café where Joan Rigby stopped most mornings for a coffee before exercising Trixie on The Stray. She was not there. Cyril went in to speak to the staff. She had not been seen that morning. They would drive to Killinghall believing she would be there.

Joan Rigby opened the door. There was neither a smile nor a bark or growl from Trixie when Ian crossed the threshold. She immediately went through to the kitchen.

"Where's Trixie?"

Joan said nothing.

Ian looked at Bennett and the female officer who had driven them to the house. "This is DCI Cyril Bennett and one of his officers. He knows just what you did to Dad."

Cyril removed the tincture bottle trapped within the plastic and held it up before her. "You know all about this, Mrs Rigby. You added the contents, a recipe developed from those given to you by your gardener, Peet, some years back. You also killed Seex. We met that day. You were a witness. I wondered why you gave your maiden name, now we know. The inexperienced officer who watched over you failed to record your details accurately but then it was a tragic traffic accident and not a murder case."

Cyril stood before her and cautioned her. "You will face trial for the murders of Seex and your husband. And then there's Stan Cooper."

She turned immediately and laughed whilst shaking her head. "Peet gave me recipes to help live a better life. You take herbal recipes daily, we all do. You drink tea and coffee, you may smoke, take aspirin, morphine if really in pain. They all come from nature, from plants. He opened my eyes to what was available here in my very own garden in Killinghall."

The word Killinghall struck home. "You didn't kill all three. You didn't actually kill Cooper. Ingrid Cooper performed that task but you produced the poison."

Immediately her manner changed. Her eyes moved, never staying focused on one spot as if she were searching for something to say.

"Talk to me, Mum. I need to know why. I need to know the truth."

She stood and went over to the tray containing the jigsaw and set it on her lap. "It starts here. My first post within this Authority. This was taken at the end of a science conference for relatively new teachers here in town. That building has gone now. Some modern apartments have replaced it. Look how beautiful the flowers are." She ran her finger over the jigsaw pressing down the occasional corner.

Four faces were missing and Cyril immediately guessed who they might be.

"See, Ian, that's me, an eager and innocent teacher and there's your father."

The faceless figure stood some distance from her.

"It's where I first met him. How handsome he was! It was only later did I notice his hands. Look carefully. They are around that girl's waist. That was your father. He would paw any girl he could but I only discovered that much, much later, when I was pregnant with you, only now I know he was worse."

Ian slipped an arm around her shoulders.

"I did get angry, Ian, and resentful but I promised myself that should I ever become really ill that I would help him to reap what he sowed. The diagnosis, the not wanting treatment was all part of the plan. I could kill those who hurt me, seriously hurt me, and then let nature be the final judge. I'm not afraid to face that trial."

Ian looked at Bennett with a tear in his eye.

"'UR/WYS 88'. That was written on the bench where your husband was found and in other places along the route he used for his daily exercise," Cyril continued.

"When I was walking Trixie, I saw him, followed him on many occasions. If I were brave enough, I'd have happily stabbed him in the back like he had done metaphorically to me so many times. The '88' is the year I truly accepted just how promiscuous he was. It is etched in my head."

"What about Seex?"

"Seex, you don't blush now, Ian, when you hear the name? You always did."

Ian nodded and attempted to match his mother's smile.

"He was a weasel, looked like one too. He started to prowl when I moved here, not that I knew that then. He knew I was a single mum. Sometimes there are moments when you're bringing up a son you need to feel human, attractive and he brought me that. He made me feel like a woman again, loved and cherished. He always said I was special, only he wasn't telling the truth. That came out when Edward Peet met Seex as well. He'd been seeing his daughter, Caroline, at the same time. He warned me. When I knew this, I used him, played him along to suit my needs." She turned to Ian. "When you left, I was alone, in a void. Not many men are interested in middle-aged frumps so I turned the tables on him and when I was diagnosed, he became the guinea pig. I didn't want to kill him straight away, that would have been too kind. I wanted to make him suffer like he made the women he chased and teased suffer and I did. That's Seex there."

There was another faceless figure set within the group.

"At the time this was taken I knew him and he became a good friend of John's but never came to the house as far as I remember. He was one of the boys, bless them. As they shut one door, they encouraged another to open it."

"There were no initials nor date found for Seex. Why was that?"

"There was, Mr Bennett, but you wouldn't find it. That was one of his sayings, usually followed by a creepy wink. I made him eat those words in the end." She looked at Cyril. "At an early meeting a record was playing in the background. We were in a café or restaurant, anyway it was *Perfect Day,* by some male singer. One of the lines was 'One day you'll reap what you sow'. He mouthed it, accompanying the song. He used it all the time after that. It was there, but as I said, you'd never find it as I made him literally eat those words in the end." She looked at the puzzled faces now staring at her. "I'd written them on a small piece of rice paper and I dropped it in the glass of my herbal tonic I insisted he drank during that breakfast. He even saw me put it in his drink and he laughed. What do you think he said? No one want to guess? These were his exact words. 'You could be adding an aphrodisiac for all I know, Joan.' And then there was that wink again and he laughed out loud before he drank it. I smiled."

"What are you saying, Mother?" Ian became extremely agitated. "Stop. You're making this up."

Cyril ignored the comment, pointing instead to the jigsaw. "I take it this missing face is Cooper's?"

"I see why you are a Chief Inspector, Mr Bennett. And that young lady there is Ingrid, Ingrid Jenson as she was then. When John left me, Ingrid was so very kind. She was non-judgemental, even when she saw me with the occasional man. It then happened to her. After that we became friends. The irony of her separation was due to Peet's daughter, she was Stan's lover. She caused them to split or so I was told. They lived close by. Funny how things come full circle. It's nature. Maybe divine intervention, who knows? When I became ill, I confided in her, told her about my desire to get revenge on some people who had been unkind in my past. To help them, as Seex always said, to reap what they sowed. We combined our ideas, made a list of all those whom we wanted to harm. It was only a game, make-believe, a laugh at first. They were all here in this puzzle I had made. It's so easy to have them done these days. Did you know that, Ian?"

"No, Mother." There was now a calm, an almost disbelieving tone to his answer.

"Initially we didn't want to kill anyone. We suffered and so would they. I suppose that one thing led to another and things got out of hand. It was after Seex and John that she asked me to kill Stan. I refused, of course."

"What about Drummond?"

"Another unpleasant and cruel individual who worked in the caring profession. He's here and there's another, Christopher Foster. You notice that he has a face. He's been saved. He'd have been the next after Drummond. How is he by the way?"

Cyril said nothing.

"I suppose you want to know how we made the poisons?"

Cyril continued to refrain from answering.

"I designed the simple process and Ingrid made it in her shed. I helped, on occasion, when her partner was out. It was his shed really, a man shed. There's another irony. I supplied the ingredients but I only had the greenhouse and it was Ingrid who offered the use of the shed."

"What of the equipment we found?" Cyril held the image of the three flasks for her to see.

"You brought me the flasks, Ian, the bottles from your father's place a year back. Do you recall? I said I wanted them for flowers. I remember when you brought them home."

A sudden cold realisation flashed across his face and he removed his arm from his mother's shoulders.

"Ingrid told me she'd added the ground crystals to Stan's flask when he was fishing. He liked a strong, Yorkshire, manly brew and she knew he'd never taste the additive. He didn't."

Cyril stood. "Joan Rigby, I am arresting you for the murder of ..." He had not completed his caution when he saw her take something from her pocket and move it to her mouth. The officer standing to her side quickly interpreted her action and grabbed her arm. Joan tried to bring her head to meet her restrained hand but she was too weak. She burst into tears.

"Please. It will allow me to go quickly and not suffer."

Her words fell on deaf ears, including those of her son.

Chapter Thirty-One

Ingrid Cooper had been placed in a holding cell. She had still failed to co-operate. April had returned to the Incident Room where Cyril joined her to go through the latest testimony from Joan Rigby.

"Little wonder we couldn't find the initials and date for Seex. That's definitely weird," April remarked.

"She wanted to be discovered," Cyril explained. "She knew she'd started something she couldn't stop."

April slid a photograph of a Sketcher shoe across the table. "It's a positive match to that found at the scene. Belongs to Ingrid Cooper."

"Bring her back into the Interview Room after I've had a word with the duty solicitor. Get her partner in here too."

Cyril and April went through Joan's statement and Cooper sat motionless. She allowed her eyes to land anywhere other than on those of her inquisitors. "What we now need to do is question your partner. He may well be up to his neck in all of this too."

"He'd nothing to do with it. Knew nothing, knows nothing."

The words shocked both April and Cyril.

"How is Joan. She's poorly, you know that? Everything she's told you is true. When we both separated from our husbands, the boys flocked like bloody vultures. John Rigby, can you believe, called on me and I know Stan dropped into Joan's when he could. For better, for worse. In sickness and in health. In health and sickness. I'm done."

"DI Richmond. If you will."

"Ingrid Cooper, I am arresting you for the murder of Paul Seex, John Rigby and Stanley Cooper and for the harm inflicted upon persons both known and at this stage unknown."

Two officers who were at the door entered, each standing by her shoulders.

"There will also be a case to answer in regard to the young mother's death."

She was led away.

Cyril and April sat back.

Nixon entered. "The poison she tried to take was a concentrated crystalline of Monkshood. It would have killed her."

"Please pass on my congratulations to PC Matford. Her quick interpretation of the situation and her swift action was key to saving Rigby. I'll be sending her a personal letter of thanks but don't tell her that. Just a pat on the back from me at this stage."

Nixon turned to go.

"And Nixon? Ian Rigby said she had a dog?"

"Found in the greenhouse asleep."

Chapter Thirty-Two

Cyril put the phone down after speaking with the Chief Constable. Someone was happy. It had been a long, yet rewarding day and he smiled. He rested his elbows on the table before unplugging an electronic cigarette. He inhaled. *It all comes from plants, the goodness and the poisons.* He remembered Joan Rigby's words clearly, inhaled and looked at his cigarette before rolling it between his fingers. Julie's words came to mind – *Nicotine is one of the most toxic of natural substances. You're still poisoning your system even in that form. I'm offering advice as someone who loves you, but remember it's your choice and yours alone.* He inhaled and allowed the mint flavour to flush his mouth before he let the steam out in one gentle exhalation. It curled as it left his mouth, twisting before spreading and gradually disappearing like morning mist. He stripped the cigarette into its different parts, unplugged the charger and dropped them into the waste bin.

Owen knocked and entered, taking a moment to look into the bin after witnessing the ceremony. "Giving up, sir?"

Cyril stood. "I am and I pity you poor buggers when my temper gets the better of me through nicotine withdrawal, but you all have broad shoulders and I'm sure you want me to live a long and tormented life."

"Well done, sir." There was little enthusiasm carried in his compliment. "We'll help. That's what mates and colleagues do. They stick together – I think. Do we still have those journals, the ones containing Rigby's recipes?"

Cyril frowned, ignoring Owen's attempt at humour, but immediately thought of the missing faces in the jigsaw. "Home. Can you drop me off?"

Cyril climbed out as Owen pulled away down West Park. He glanced across at the Turnpike stone and then at the pub. He could kill a pint. He would nip in for a half and then go home. Fortunately, the bar was quiet.

Owen parked in his dedicated spot allocated to his apartment. The evening was still warm. To his surprise Hannah's car was missing and so he finished listening to the radio news, anticipating she would return at any moment. She should normally be home at this time. Collecting his jacket from the back seat, he crossed the car park. The hall light was on, it was never turned off unless they were both in. Tossing his keys into the crap bowl, he went directly to the fridge. Attached to the door by a magnet was a note.

Knew this would be your first port of call. Picnic packed, bring a coat. You, my darling man, are my idol. Meet me at the place of your two-hundred-ton Idol. You're supposed to be a detective but as I don't want to eat this picnic on my own, please think before you drive! Love you xx I left at 4.35!

As you're only an Inspector – Rock on! – Another clue!
xxHxx

He checked his watch. Thirty minutes ago. She might just be arriving at Brimham Rocks. Owen grabbed a couple of fleece jackets, a torch, not that it was near dusk, and a lump of cheese from the fridge to eat on the way. He decided to leave the pickled onion. He calculated the quickest route to Hannah was via Bedlam; the satnav showed a twenty-minute drive.

Hannah's car was in the car park along with many more. As it was such a glorious day he knew it would be busy. Grabbing the jackets, he set off. A few people passed him and he could hear children's laughter as they climbed on some of the first rock formations close to the path. The Idol, his rock, was probably the furthest from the lower car park. The walk would take him five minutes.

As he approached, Hannah was sitting just away from the central rock. She had spread a tartan blanket on the ground; a small basket covered with a cloth was positioned centrally. She spotted him and Owen waved as he climbed the last part of the sloping dirt path that led to the small plateau where the Idol stood. He spread his hands.

"I don't understand. It's not my birthday and I hope to goodness it's not yours. No, it's definitely not, that's January 30th."

Hannah tapped the blanket next to her. He followed her direction and went and sat down.

"Brought you a fleece just in case." Owen put one round her shoulders.

"I did too. I'm sitting on it." She kissed him before peeling back the checked cloth that covered the basket. Positioned in the centre was a large Appleton's pork pie, some plates, napkins and cutlery and two bottles of Black Sheep Ale.

His face lit up. "You really know how to spoil a man,

Hannah Peters."

"Ordered and then collected on my way through Ripon. Took me longer than I thought."

He leaned to take one of the bottles. "You still not drinking?"

She shook her head. "Sparkling water."

Owen pulled a face as if she'd uttered a rude word. "You know what fish do in water, don't you, young lady?"

She chuckled. "Swim?"

"Here's a clue for you. Kids drank ale in the olden days because the water was so crap for want of a better word and that was before fluoride and chlorine!" He emphasised the word *crap*. "With me?" Taking the top off the first bottle he was just about to take a drink. "This is a great idea. We should do it more often. I love surprises."

Hannah moved the bottle from his lips. "Just a minute. I've got something to tell you."

Owen brought the bottle down and trapped it between his legs. "Have I done something wrong?" His face showed real concern. "Have I missed an anniversary?"

"No … You're going to be a father. Tests came back yesterday. Julie confirmed them. Hence, I've not been drinking these last few days or so, detective."

The scream of an excited child somewhere over to their left broke the silence but echoed amongst the ancient crags.

"Say that again."

"We, my handsome man, we have made a new life. We are going to be a mum and dad. Although I said I wasn't sure about being a parent, well that's just gone out of the window. I couldn't be happier. I can't wait!"

Owen leaned over, grabbed her and kissed her more passionately and for longer than he believed he had ever kissed her before. Tears of joy ran down his cheeks as the beer dribbled over his legs.

"You special, special girl, the mother of our child. I love you more than that bloody rock."

Hannah looked at the rock and back at Owen but took it in the spirit in which it was meant.

"If only Gran and Grandad were alive. God they'd be so, so happy. Can I ring Cyril?"

Hannah nodded. "Julie promised me she wouldn't say anything. Go on. You were his best man and he deserves to know first. But before you do, pick up your beer, if it's not all over your trouser legs and the rug. Cheers, handsome, and thank you for picking me. To us and the lump."

More tears rolled down his cheeks as he felt for his phone. He tried to dial but he was all fingers and thumbs. Hannah took it and dialled before handing it back. It rang three times.

"Bennett!" Cyril answered in his usual brusque way.

"Sir, it's Owen."

"Fancy coming for a beer, Owen?"

"No, sir, I've got one. Sir," he paused trying to get the correct words, "we are going to be a dad ... no sorry, Hannah's not, she's not going to be a dad, she's going to be the mum. I am, me, David Owen. I'm going to be a father!"

Malcolm Hollingdrake

Featured Artist

Bernard Walter Evans
26th December 1843 – 26th February 1922

Bernard Evans lived in Harrogate from the late 1880s until about 1911, residing at 20 Park Parade. Researching this artist, I realised he lived overlooking the church near where Dr John Rigby's body was discovered. It never ceases to amaze me how often these coincidences occur.

Evans was born in Wolverhampton and studied painting in Birmingham from the age of seven under the direction of Samuel Lines, William Wallis and Edward Watson. Evans became a prolific landscape painter, in both oil and watercolour mostly depicting the Midlands, Yorkshire and North Wales. He also painted in the South of France around Cannes, exhibiting many times throughout the United Kingdom. His first exhibition was at the Royal Birmingham Society of Artists in 1864. He exhibited at the Royal Academy on thirteen occasions.

Evans was the cousin of the author George Eliot (Mary Ann Evans).

Many of his paintings depicting Yorkshire are beautifully detailed.

Malcolm Hollingdrake

Acknowledgements

And then the sun took a step back, the leaves lulled
themselves to sleep and autumn was awakened.
Raquel Franco

We come to the close of another chapter in the Harrogate Crime Series. This book came about through the purchase at auction of a book entitled, "Deadly Doses: A Writer's Guide to Poisons". It was sold by Caroline Maston as part of an online auction to raise money for her school. It has remained on the shelf for a year or so but it proved invaluable as research for this book.

I always try to keep a record of all those who have helped in the writing of my books.

A massive thanks to Gary Barton for his scientific support. I could not have written this book without you. I know nothing about fly fishing and help was at hand through Geoff Blakesley, a keen angler who not only gave detailed descriptions of the sites, but also sent a set photographs of him dressed in the appropriate clothing. Thank you. Gordon McGregor, a college friend who taught for many years in North Yorkshire and shared his knowledge of the internal plan of the Harrogate Teachers' Centre. It is vital to have these first-hand accounts even when writing fiction.

Breaking two teeth on an almond was not the best thing

I could have done but the experience proved most useful and inspirational ... nothing is wasted, all is stored to be used somewhere along the writing road.

Again, my thanks to Kevin Graham for the fabulous cover photograph and to Craig Benyon of Create Print, Wigan for his work on the cover designs.

Once the writing is completed many hours of work still remain. To Debbie, my wife, who lost one of her brothers during this process but battled on and I am grateful, as always, for her commitment to my writing. Helen Gray who checks every word, thank you. To my advanced readers, Gill and Ian Cleverdon, Carrie Heap and Lynda Checkley, Donna Morfett, Craig Gillan, Dee Groocock, Kath Middleton, Samantha Brownley, Lucy Sampson, Donna Wilbor, Susan Hunter, Christopher Nolan, Emma Truelove and Sarah Hardy. Thank you. To Caroline Vincent – you know the role you played in the writing of this book. I'm grateful.

I have loved adding the names of people I know to characters. I hope you were surprised to see yourself in 'Fragments'.

There are also many other people who support the series, the bloggers, the reading groups, who offer guidance and masses of encouragement. You are all the wind beneath many an author's wings. Remember you are greatly appreciated.

It is, however, to you, dear reader who has chosen this book from the countless thousands available for whom I reserve my final thanks. Without you, there would be very little point in picking up my pen. Thank you.

Finally. **SPOILER ALERT.** I would love you to review this book, either by just allocating the stars you feel it deserves or by adding a few words. Please do not mention Owen's lovely news. Keep it secret so that others can stumble on it and be surprised. Thank you!

Until Book 11.

Malcolm

If you enjoy this series, I have a new collection published by Hobeck Books. 'Catch as Catch Can' and 'Syn' will be available from April and May this year.

If you would like further details then you can always find me on:

www.malcolmhollingdrakeauthor.co.uk

www.malcolmhollingdrakeauthor.com

Fragments

Printed in Great Britain
by Amazon